The Learning

The Learning

By Ty Hamilton

1st edition, Published 2016

Printed in the United States of America.

Library of Congress Control Number: 2016910459

The Learning/Ty Hamilton – 1st edition
First Printing: 2016

ISBN-10: 0-9977399-0-8

ISBN-13: 978-0-9977399-0-9

www.TheLearningNovel.com

Thank you to the beautiful lady on my front cover:

Sissy's daughter, my 2nd cousin

Kiana

DEDICATION

I want you to know it is very hard to feel the fear of not being accepted and putting your work out for others to critique, but I have faith! I wrote these books to reach my Universal family. I hope that you will remember thru it all, all we ever had as a people was God and family!

For me, my Nana sits at the right hand of his throne. She taught me about Him. Even though you can call him by any name, there is only one true God. My Nana taught me about unconditional love, and as dysfunctional as we may be, we are family and I love all of you.

To my mother Ruth, I hope I make you proud. To my Uncle Homer, aka Uncle David, it is my honor to be your favorite niece. To Aunt Pam and Daddy Bruce, thank you for your support. Pam, you are my biggest fan. To my sweet Aunt Judy aka Judith, we go way back. You are the secret to my smile.

To my cousins Shari, Dennis, and Kip, (Kip you know who you are), I grew up with you. You are more than my cousins; you are my brothers and my sister Shari, aka Sissy!

To Aleisha, Crystal, Jackie and your sons and daughters; thank you so much for trusting me and believing in me. Aleisha you and I have a special bond!

To my son Timothy, you encourage me. You are loved and thank you for loving me.

But most importantly, thank you to My Heavenly Father, my Lord and Savior. I wish I could reach up to the heavens and give you a Big Hug. All my life, you and only you, have been my light. I love you for all you are and for being the only Father I have ever known. Thank you, Jesus!

INTRODUCTION

One hundred and ten years ago Nana Montague, the Matriarch of the Montague family, was enslaved on the very plantation she now owns. Nana went from slave to **Billionaire**!

At the age of ten, Nana witnessed the savage murder of her Father and the selling of her Mother. Even though she felt helpless, she could read and write; and she wrote every tragedy and heartbreaking events in detail in a book she calls:
THE LEARNING!

With one phone call, Nana has requested her grandchildren to come home. They must do what she can't. They must accept their destiny and get their
LEARNING.

Cousins, Teresa and Steven Montague are the catalysts for the future of the Montagues. This is the first time gifted male and female Bamileke Warriors exist in this country, and their **GIFTS** are extraordinary! Accompanying them on their journeys are their cousins: Kip, Dennis, and Sissy.

These Modern Day Warriors believe in God first, family second, an eye for an eye and never bargain with the devil! So with this unpredictable team, they will take what is theirs, protect their family, their land and write their new chapters into

THE LEARNING!

CHAPTER 1 – The Phone Call

It is 3:00 am and Teresa Montague (Mon ta Que) (Ty as her family calls her) is wide awake and sitting in front of two big-screen monitors. Her office is filled with cushion travel cases with audio and visual equipment. A huge vision board is covered with vital information and inspirational quotes to keep her focused on her goals.

A Business license and seven copyrights fill the walls, and a big screen television provides the right amount of distractions to keep her informed.

Unexpectedly the phone rings and a familiar feeling of dread flashes over her body. Phone calls at 3:00 am only mean one thing, someone died or is about to die!

"Hello," Ty said with hesitation.

"Hello, I'm trying to reach Teresa Montague," Judith said.

"This is she and with whom am I speaking to?" Ty asked.

"Ooh sweetheart this is Ms. Judith, your grandmother's caregiver. She asked me to call you and the others. It's almost time; almost time for her to go and she needs you all here for The Learning."

"Ms. Judith you're telling me, my Nana is dying and she wants us there for The Learning?' Ty asked.

"Yes, sweetheart that's what she said, The Learning," Judith stated.

"Dear God, Ms. Judith I'll contact my cousins and we'll be there immediately. Please tell Nana I love her and I'm on my way." Ty said.

"Ok Baby, God's speed," Judith said as they hung up the phone.

***

The phone rang three times and Kip picked it up.

"Yo, it's 3:10 in the morning and this better be the right number." He said.

"Kip, it's your cousin Ty. I just got a call about Nana.

She wants us all to come home ASAP, It's about that time." Ty said.

"Damn, I always know by these dreadful three in the morning phone calls someone died or is going to die." He said.

"Yo cuz, you driving in?" Kip asked.

"Yeah, you know Florida is eight to nine hours away from Louisiana." she said.

"Can you bring Luis' boat?" Kip asked.

"Damn this ain't no vacation Kip," she shouted.

"Oh come on! The Mississippi is across the street from Nana's home." Kip said.

"Bye Kip, see you soon." She said.

"Bye baby girl," Kip said as he hung up the phone.

***

It was time to call Shari, but family lovingly called her by her nickname, Sissy. The phone rang twice and a very alert Shari answered.

"Hello," Sissy said with panicked in her voice.

"Hello, Sissy this is Ty. Nana called and she wants us all in Louisiana, ASAP."

"I had a feeling," Sissy said.

"Sissy please don't start that!" Ty said.

"Girl you know all about it and don't act like you don't. I'll call Dennis' wild ass and I'll get up out of Ohio on the first thing smoking." Sissy said.

"Love you Sissy." Ty said.

"I love you too Ty."

***

Ty got up from her desk and headed to the kitchen to start a pot of coffee.

"Well, there's no sense in trying to go to

sleep. We have got to pack up and load up," Ty said as she looked at two full grown black Rottweilers named Rock and Scotty. "We're going to see Nana! So let's go wake up Luis." She said.

Ty headed to the master bedroom with dogs in tow. She leaned over and kissing an aged but handsome beard and Luis woke up. Luis Miguel Rivera opened his eyes and spoke with a thick Spanish accent:

"Mamita, what time is it?" Luis asked.

"It's 3:45 in the morning." Ty said.

"You trying to love me to death?" he asked.

"No," Ty said half smiling, "it's Nana, she's dying and she wants us to come home. I have a feeling it's going to take a while because she said it's time for The Learning."

"The Learning?" Luis asked.

"Yes, The Learning, now get up and let's get packed. Oh, you need to hook up the boat." She said.

"The Boat?" Luis asked curiously.

"That's Kip! You're from New York by way of Puerto Rico, and every time you get near water you've got to get in the boat." Ty said.

"Kip has a way of making a good time out of a funeral," Luis replied with a laugh. "Ok Ty, let's get it."

***

Luis was driving his truck with Scotty in the front seat and a large boat attached to the back. Ty was driving her SUV with Rock by her side, as she talked to Luis hands-free on her cell phone.

"We just entered the Louisiana city limits and there are ten miles to go." Ty said.

"This reminds me when we came here to visit." responded Luis.

"I know and I can't believe Nana owns the plantation our ancestors were enslaved on. It is one hundred thousand acres of crops, orchards, livestock and undeveloped land. Oh and a huge family cemetery. Luis, this plantation was built in 1860, that's one hundred and fifty-five years ago, and Nana is one hundred and ten years old."

"You know, to look into her eyes, I have a feeling this is the time period we are going to cover in The Learning." Ty said.

"I think you're right. You'll know for sure in a few more miles." Luis said.

***

They saw the sign on the right that said, "You

are entering Private Property, The Montague Planta-tion." At the bottom in Kip's handwriting, it said: **"If you are not a Montague, you are not welcome."**

They both laughed in synch and said, "That damn Kip."

The sun was going down as they pulled up to the black cast iron ten-foot gate. It was flanked on both sides with white bricks and huge initials span-ning the center of the gate that read: **K N M**.

"Nana had those initials changed seventy years ago. They are her Mother and Father's initials, Kimtu and Nettie Montague," Ty said.

"Hard to believe little old Nana owns all of this," as soon as he said it the gate slowly opened on its own accord.

Neither one of them said a thing as they drove to the Mansion up ahead.

The road was lined with magnolia, poplar and oak trees, and you could make out a white Antebellum Mansion, black cast iron balconies and a huge round water fountain in the center of the circular driveway.

"This place is so alive. Just like I remembered growing up," Ty said.

"Yes it is and I wonder who maintains it and collects the harvest," Luis said.

"You really know how to crush my moment. Nana is extremely intelligent and I'm sure she has a crew and a method that works. After all Luis, she has been here and only here all of her life." Ty said.

"You mean Nana has never left this plantation?" Luis asked.

"Born into slavery here and will die a free woman here. This is her home, and I don't have a clue as to how she came to own it.

All I know is Nana is the last original slave of this plantation." Ty explained.

Both vehicles pulled around the circular driveway and parked. As they exited with two dogs by their side, they looked up to the second-floor balcony. She was standing, with the assistance of an African wooden cane, **Nana!**

Her skin the color of caramel, features keen and strong, slightly aged, with thick, salt and pepper loose curled hair that flowed to her hips. Yessss, above them, stood five foot, one inch, one hundred and ten years old, **Nana!**

She looked down at them and smiled. With her perfect white teeth and clear beautiful gray eyes, **Nana Montague!**

***

CHAPTER 2 - What Nana Wants?

After the hugs and kisses, Ms. Judith served dinner. They were sitting at the formal table with all the fresh harvest in front of them: collard greens, candied yams, smoked ham, fried chicken, cornbread so thick it looked like cake, dripping with freshly churned butter, corn on the cob, sweet potato pies covered with fresh pecans and lemon pound cake. Just as they finished with grace, Kip, Sissy, and Dennis pulled into the driveway.

"They're right on time for dinner!" Nana said.

Kip, Dennis, and Sissy loaded into the house and hugged and kissed everyone. They were hungry and ready to eat.

The homemade wine was poured and a loud joyful conversation ensued.

***

Now that dinner was done, it was time for the conversation they all wanted to hear:

"Children, help me to the living room and gather around the fireplace," Nana said.

"Dennis go get Nana that book, right over there," Nana said.

Dennis asked, "This book Nana, the one wrapped in this funny looking cloth?"

"Yes child, that one. It's time for The Learning to begin. Luis, I'm sorry Hun, but this is for Montagues only." Nana said.

"Ok Nana, I'll help Ms. Judith in the kitchen and unpack the car," Luis said.

"Come on children gather round and listen well. This book is the history of our lives as we know it here on this soil. I warn you don't talk about this to anyone that is not of our bloodline. No One!" Nana said.

As Nana looked at each of them, there was an understanding as clear as the words she just spoke, and nothing else needed to be said.

"Dennis, this funny looking cloth was the linen cloth my Father wore when he was kidnapped from Africa. It is the only thing we have from our homeland besides the tribal markings that were on his upper right shoulder."

"My Father was a Bamileke. The Bamileke are from an area known as the Cameroon Grasslands of Africa. They are farmers and they also raise animals," she said.

"The women are believed to make the soil more fruitful, so they are responsible for planting and harvesting crops. The men clear the land and hunt. We recognize SI as the Supreme God and honor our ancestors. We believe our ancestor's spirits are embodied in the skulls. Not all of the ancestor's skulls are with us. Those that are not, well we pour out Spirits, liquor on the ground. You know like Snoopy Dog does for his homeys that have passed away." Nana is trying to relate causing everyone to smile.

"Then the dirt gathered from the spot looks like the skull of our loved ones.

One last thing, a Bamileke would rather die or go to war than to be enslaved!" Nana said.

"So Nana your Father was kidnapped?" Kip asked.

"Yes, he was betrayed by a friend and led to the slave traders. My Father fought for his life but he was knocked out and taken against his will. He never spoke of the journey to this country but the look on his face spoke fathoms." She said.

"Father was very weak when they brought him here or else I'm sure he would have been able to sink the ship or taken some other drastic measures, other than being a slave. It must have been Hell, a living Hell." She said.

Nana *mentally* flashed back to her Father being brought to the auction blocks and bided on like an animal. An aristocratic white man stepped up and bided the most. He had bought himself a slave, but not really, Father was a Bamileke Warrior.

"My Father was brought to this place as a slave. A Warrior that would rather die and start a war than to be a slave! And start a war, is just what he did. Father rounded up all the able body men to revolt and burn this plantation down to the ground." Nana said.

"But his plans were foiled by an old slave that knew no other way but slavery. He couldn't see past this life. I feel sorry for that stupid nigga, stupid indeed."

"The night of the revolt, Father and his men were ambushed by the Master of this plantation. They fought for their lives and killed as many of them as they could before being taken. As the leader, Father fared the worst. I'll never forget, I wrote everything down, everything he taught me, everything I saw and

I was only ten years old."

"It took four men to tie him to the whipping post. They whipped him till no place on him was untouched. The sight of it forced unnatural chills down my spine. I had never seen a man beat so violently and his back cut open to reveal his actual spine. His screams, his screams, I can still hear his screams."

"Understand me children, Father was a big man, strong and would fight till the end but the human body can only take so much torture. They made all his children watch everything they did to him, all nine of us and my Mother Nettie. I knew my mind snapped when Father's screams changed to begging for mercy."

"My Mother's screams went silent when she saw them cut off Father's manhood. Somehow she knew they were going to kill him and I did too!" she said.

Nana wiped the tears from her eyes as Kip, Ty, Dennis and Sissy stood right there with her. They saw it too. Scene for scene they cried and flinched with every swing of the whip as all four men whipped him one lash after the other. They physically saw it… they were getting The Learning but how could they be seeing this?

"Ooh my," as Nana looked at all their eyes. "Your eyes…your eyes are all glowing gray, just like Father's was. That's why they covered him with a burlap sack. Father had gone silent and his eyes were glowing white gray. Just like yours. It's that gift that scared them. Father said we all had it and I know that to be true." Nana said.

"Father was lifting big old oak trees with his mind, and the lighter his eyes got the more the earth shook. That's why they put them out…and covered his head with that sack…his eyes…they put them out." She said.

"Montague, himself, took his thumbs and push into Father's eye. He pushed with so much force till Mother and I saw blood and fluids spewed out of Father's eyes. I don't know how I watched and didn't turn away. It was all too surreal. I couldn't turn away. I had to see it all. Every uncivilized, barbaric thing they did to him, but even with all that, he was not dead! He was still alive when they put him in a boat on the river over there and I followed them."

"They tied him up with full feed sacks so he would stay down. Then they threw Father in the river, right by that big old tree."

"I just couldn't look anymore. When I closed my eyes, I heard my father say: little one, be strong and hold our family together. Somehow, someway you will see freedom and we will never be enslaved again. Tell your children of me and never forget what I have taught you. I love you, beyond this life."

"Then he went silent. **Oh God, I tried to lift him up but I couldn't! My gift was not as strong as his. I feel him…he's still there. We have to bring him home; him and the rest of them. We have to and lay them all to rest!**" she yelled.

Nana stopped and her head fell forward and so did theirs. Everyone saw what Nana had seen that night and all of them were crying and gasping for air.

"We brought the boat, Nana. And tomorrow, we'll bring him home." Ty said.

"Yes child, we gonna bring him home!" Nana said.

CHAPTER 3 - Bringing Father home

When the rooster crowed, everyone woke up. Today is the day. Ty was downstairs making coffee and breakfast as everyone assembled at the table.

"Luis, today we are in need of your boat. We're gonna bring my Father home," Nana said.

"Of course Nana, but I thought he was deceased," Luis replied.

"He is, but we're bringing him home today to lay him to rest. For one hundred years my Father has been at the bottom of the Mississippi River. Right over there by that big tree." Nana said.

"Ay mi Dios, Nana are you sure? His body must be horrifying. Can all of you handle the way...?" Luis asked.

As Nana cut him off, "whatever we see, it must be done and we must bring him home and lay him to rest. I'm counting on my children to do it. I can't, but they can. It is time to embrace your gift children and know that this is only the beginning of The Learning." Nana said.

Kip, Ty, Sissy and Dennis looked at each other and their gray eyes flashed as they winked, and rose up from the table. Kip and Luis went outside to get the boat ready. Ms. Judith prepared Nana to go to the river, as Sissy and Ty put on their swimsuits. Dennis was standing at the front door looking out at the river, quiet and eerie, and he has never been quiet.

Everyone exited the house and entered the truck and boat. Dennis got into the driver's seat as Luis and Kip kept Nana secure in the boat. Sissy and Ty joined Dennis in the truck and they were off.

Instinctively, Dennis drove thru the opening gates, across the street, and into the woods before seeing the massive river ahead.

"Luis, you will drive this boat to where I tell you, understood? When we get there you will turn your back away from us. I don't want you to bare witness to what you could not understand." Nana said.

"Yes, Ma'am," Luis said.

***

As Dennis backed the boat into the water, Nana clinched her wooden African cane. Kip gave him the signal to stop and Sissy and Ty jumped in the boat and sat next to Nana. Kip and Dennis released the boat into the water and Luis started the engine, then they joined Nana in the boat and all four of them turned and faced her.

"Children all of you must enter the water and swim towards the big tree. You will know when to dive under. Keep your eyes open, they will give you light to see in this mucky water. Kip and Dennis, you will need these knives to free him. Take him to the barn and I will meet you there." Nana said.

"Yes Nana," they said.

At the stern, Luis did exactly as Nana

instructed. Down the river in front of the big tree, he dropped anchor and turned off the engine. He turned his back to them, poured himself a large glass of Puerto Rican rum and lit a Cuban cigar.

"May God be with us all," Luis said.

They all turned to look at Nana; she was not relaxed as usual. She was recalling that night, one hundred years ago as a ten-year-old girl, helpless and trying with all her might to help her Father, but she could only watch. After seeing her thoughts, one after the other, they slid off the boat into the water and begin to swim towards the big tree. Nana watched her synchronized swimmers take a deep breath and dive deep into the dirty Mississippi.

As they opened their eyes, bright gray light cut through the thick muck and they could see clear as day. Five feet ahead of them they all stopped, they saw him! All six foot five inches, an expansive mass covered in a tan brown stained and aged burlap sack. He had full feed bags on his chest and legs, tied with a heavy green rope. The river plants had grown over him and they swayed with the rhythm of the current of the great Mississippi River. His body was not touching the bottom of the river bed. Even though they were at least twelve feet down, he was parallel to the bottom, facing upward in a plank position without support under his back, like a pharaoh, minus the golden sarcophagus.

As one, they headed straight up to fill their lungs and then they dove down directly to him. Kip and Dennis reached him first, as Sissy and Ty supplied bright gray light. They quickly cut away the plants and the rope. Carefully, they lifted the feed bags off of his body, and then he began to rise.

With Kip and Dennis behind him, one on each side, and Sissy and Ty in front of him; he followed them up until they all surfaced at the same time. Without touch, but eyes blazing gray, they swam in formation, like warriors carrying one of their fallen.

Not one word was exchanged as Nana watched in amazement. Her Father remained in plank position as these four Warriors *mentally* lifted his huge body from the water to the shore. Without touch, but by using their minds as one, these fearless Warriors worked together.

Luis was watching them, "Nana my God, did you see that? Jesus Lord I need a drink!" he said.

Nana was clapping and now standing. "Together, my children have amazing gifts."

"I knew. I knew they would bring him home. Luis give Nana a drink and then let's go!" she said.

***

Nana and Luis drove slowly behind Kip and Dennis, while Ty and Sissy walked to the front gate that was already opening on its own. As they walked, the water never stopped flowing from the burlap sack. It was purging from his body and his girth was reducing. His body was taking the form of a man, forty-five years in age, built like the African warrior he once was.

Nana's eyes glowed solid gray as she smiled and said out loud, "take him to the barn children. We will ready him for burial tomorrow. Father, we own this land and always will. I will bury you and Mother together at the head of the cemetery. All your children and their children will be buried there as a family. Kimtu Bouso you can rest. Rest in peace my loving Father, you are home with us."

***

Kimtu lay on a wooden table cushioned with blankets and a pillow beneath his head. His body was at its normal size. The water had completed its purge, and Kip and Dennis removed the burlap sack that covered his face and entombed him.

Before them laid a forty-five-year-old man, with the color of rich ebony African soil. He had keen warrior chisel features, straight nose, small lips and a head of jet black loose spiral curls that fell to his shoulders. A full black beard shaded his oval face and his eyebrows were perfectly groomed, as the arch of them formed at the ends.

The tattered clothing that lay flat on his strong, tall, muscular physique was being gently re-moved by Sissy; as Ty bathed his skin and Nana rubbed him softly with palm oil. It was healing oil that closed every wound and rejuvenated the missing flesh. Dennis stood at the end of the table with his gray eyes glowing slightly, as if to warm Father's skin and add to the healing process. They all could see their Great Grandfather was a beautiful Bamileke Warrior!

***

No more scares, no evidence of the horrific night his body had endured. Finally his eyes, Nana opened his right eyelid and exposed what was left. It resembled a broken poached egg. She gasped and dropped the eyelid and pushed back away from him. Sissy immediately took her place and lifted the lid. She and Ty softly glowed gray light into it. Even though it regenerated, it weakened them.

Kip and Dennis began the procedure in his left

eye all the way to restoration, and it didn't faze their gift.

Then Nana stepped up, as they moved back. She raised both lids and removed her hands.

Both eyes were rolled back to the white pupils, but Nana's eyes glowed gray light on his and they rolled forward to expose soft gray eyes, as bright and pretty as God's colors mixed in the clouds on a partially sunny day.

They all smiled as if looking at a new born baby. Finally, Nana covered him to his waist with a sparkling white sheet.

"Thank you children, we're almost done and my Father will finally rest in peace," Nana said.

His eyelids closed and any sign of pain or struggle left his face, as he lay there in stasis, awaiting his burial. Actually, he looked as if he was sleeping peacefully.

The family moved towards the barn door as it opened on its own, and the lights inside began to go out leaving only the one over him, as it dimmed to a soft yellow glow. Looking back, their gray eyes glowed a soft gentle beam over him. Then they turned and left and the barn door softly closed behind them.

***

Returning to the mansion, they were all in their rooms; bathing and enjoying the gumbo Ms. Judith had prepared for them. But instead of eating, Luis was staring at Ty as if she was repulsive.

"Ty, what are you? What you did today, dear God, all of you, what are *you* people?" Luis asked in terror.

"You want ta watch that, *you people* shit. Do

you have any idea what I could do to you? You liar! You know what Luis, I want you to go home but not to my house. I want you to go home to the woman you have been sleeping with for the last year, the one that has your baby. Believe me; you don't want to take anything of mine. You have already taken too much of me, as is." Ty said.

"Don't mess with my money. Just get your shit and get the hell out," she said as she looked up at him with her eyes full blazed!

"If it wasn't a sin, I would tie you down with full feed bags and throw your ass in the Mississippi River. Do you hear me?" Ty asked.

Luis was paralyzed with fear after what he just saw today and the fact that she knew every detail of his lie of a life.

"I think it would be best if I did go." he said.

"Best! You better get the hell out of my Nana's house!" Ty yelled.

Luis rattled the keys to the truck and backed out the room never taking his eyes off of Ty. Pure fear gushed through his veins causing his chest to pound. He damn near ran down the stairs, but he missed the first step and fell on his ass and slid the length of the staircase all the way down to the double front doors.

Ty was watching him the whole time with her *mind's eye.* She giggled when he hit the bottom of the stairs with a thud. M*entally* she opened the big wooden front doors and he heard her voice say:

"Get the hell out. You've taken enough from me so don't take anything of mine."

As he ran through the front doors Rock and Scotty were there in attack mode with their fangs dropped and snarling. He heard Ty's wicked laugh. It was as if she was controlling them. They backed him off the porch slowly but never once taking their eyes off him. Like wolves stalking their prey, they encircled him to move in one direction, towards the truck.

Luis ran for his life, jumped into the truck and did seventy miles per hour down the driveway with the boat attached to the back.

His precious boat bounced from left to right as if it was going to detach itself at any time. The cast iron gates were already open for his exit, and the sign that was on the right coming in was now on his right as he was going out.

It read: You are leaving the Montague properties. And in Ty's handwriting at the bottom, it said: **"If you're not a Montague, don't bring your ass up in here!"**

Nana and Kip got the giggles as they had watched the whole thing in their *mind's eye.*

"Oh, she's a Montague," Nana spoke out loud.

"For life Nana, for life," Kip said.

***

CHAPTER 4 - The Gift

He is the best alarm clock in the world." Ty stated as the rooster crowed. Ms. Judith was downstairs cooking crab cakes, grits, and homemade biscuits. She sliced up fresh peaches, straight out the orchard and served them up with heavy crème, whipped into a fluffy cloud. Breakfast was delicious and they enjoyed themselves and conversed joyfully on this beautiful day.

After all, at dusk they will bury Father at the head of the cemetery; and he will never be moved from his final resting place, never! But till then, it was time for The Learning.

"Dennis child, get Nana the Learning book and tell the others to meet up in the Library," Nana said.

Nana entered the library to find everyone there just waiting for their next lesson.

"I'm sure you all are wondering about your gift and what you can do with it. Your gift comes with great responsibility. You have the right to protect yourself, your family, your home. Do not use your gift for revenge. Vengeance belongs to SI! Use it for good and good will return to you. Use it for bad or in anger and you will have to repent to SI.

Understood children?" Nana asked.

"Understood, Nana," They all replied.

"First let me tell you what your gift is not. It's not voodoo or witchcraft. It's like when a man loses his sense of sight. The energy goes to his other senses and they are sharper, more acute."

"We have five senses too, but you children have the ability to cut off all the energy to your other senses and direct that energy to your brain."

"With your brains, you can move without touch, talk without speaking, see without seeing and hear without hearing. The more energy to your brain the more the neurons fire and the electricity from the neurons show bright light thru your gray eyes. All of this is done because you have the ability to concentrate far greater than others and control that energy. We all have this gift, but the third generation, first child has the ability to link."

"Yes, link all these gifts together and that means amazing things. Have you not noticed there is no talking, no hearing, and no touching when you are on a mission? Everything is instinctive!" Nana asked.

"Nana what do you mean by the third generation, first child," Kip asked?

"Well child, my Father was the third generation, first child of his Mother and Father.

"I am my Father's first generation, eighth child. My children are second generation and my children's children..You... are the third generation. Kip, you are third generation, first child and Sissy and Dennis are third generation, second and third child. They have the gift like we all do but Kip; you have the ability to link." Nana said.

"But Nana, I'm third generation, first child, an

only child." Ty said.

"You got something extra. You can link and do something special," Nana said. "Now listen children, I had three sons and two daughters. There are three more third generations, first child; two men and one woman."

"Unfortunately, a man-child and the woman-child died. So that leaves one man left, like Kip and he will be joining us soon, because children, we have a lot to do." Nana said.

Their eyes were fixed on Nana and filled with more questions. Nana knows she must feed them more of The Learning.

"Y'all got to stop rushing questions to my brain. I hear you, where's my husband, how did I get this place, who is Ms. Judith and on and on. Nana's old so we gonna have to take this one step at a time.

Let's start with how I got this place, but first, I need some coffee and lemon cake. Children it's a beautiful day, so let's get some fresh air and sit on the front porch." She said.

***

Nana was sitting on the long southern porch in her favorite rocker with The Learning Book on her lap.

"Ooh children, Nana haven't had such a wonderful day like this in a long time." she said.

"Nana please, back to The Learning," Dennis said. "How did you become the owner of the Montague Plantation?" he asked.

Nana said with a laugh, "Child, we have to go back to the civil war when Mr. Montague went off to fight against the North. Oh, he came back, minus an arm and a leg. His daughter Karen, got the fever and died. Mrs. Montague couldn't have any more children after Karen. So they made me her slave companion and I got my teachings from her." Nana said as she gave them a slick smile.

"Mrs. Montague was a bitter, cynical, ugly woman. She had the money in the family and that's why he married her. So the midwife kinda fixed her, right after birth, and she got hers. You know children; slaves had a way to get at you."

"It was stupid to put them in your household, cooking your food and taking care of your children. The slaves were stronger and smarter and white folks got weaker and arrogant. They were dependent on us to wipe their asses." She said with a smile. "Weak and arrogant." She repeated to make her point.

"Karen taught me everything she learned in school, even French. Child, Nana read every book in their library. I got myself the equivalent of a Master's degree in business with a minor in Accounting. Yes, I'm a smart African, just look around." She said.

"I knew it! Dennis never listens to me. He got them big ears, but he doesn't hear a thing." Sissy said.

"Sissy, he's been that way all his life," Nana said as she smiled at Dennis and he smiled back.

"Anyway, back to The Learning children. Karen died, Mrs. Montague lost what little mind she had and Mr. Montague came back a half a man, literally.

"Mrs. Montague spent her time running around naked talking about she was a slave and we were her Masters. She didn't know how right she was. Because of the war we were considered free, and all the slaves stayed. They stayed just because I asked them to. I couldn't leave, not with Father still here. Anyway, I had my mind on owning what rightfully belonged to us. For all we had lost and given to these people, they were gonna give it back, tenfold."

"Children when I tell you the Northern Soldiers tore this plantation down and these weak people too; it was the best payback ever. SI said vengeance is his...ooh he had to be mad as hell. I told my people do not rebuild this plantation, no, not yet, and they listened. I told them we are survivors but they aren't. It was time to root them out." Nana said.

"We put the Montagues in the worst slave's quarters because the big house was burned up and lying in bricks after the cannon fire and raids. The fields were a wreck; the orchards were overgrown with fruit rotting on the ground. We fed them the slop they had fed us for years. We left them to lay in their waste for days. We told them we had to look for food and all we could find was very little."

"See Nana had a plan, because it came to me clear as day. The Montague's had no descendants, no one to inherit this land. So why not me?" she asked.

"I would buy this land from him for what it was worth in its dilapidated state. I would offer to take care of them till the day they died, but he had to deed this whole plantation to us." She said.

***

"Now we worked the gardens around the slave quarters, hunted for animals to eat and sire other animals. We took our products to the market and sold them dirt cheap, as not to be noticed. Slowly we made forty dollars." She said.

"So after months of eating slop and laying around in their own fifth, Mr. Montague demanded we bathe him and take care of his crazy ass wife. I told him, oh no, we were free and if he wanted us to, we would leave. We would leave him and his wife to fend for themselves. Mr. Montague laughed in my face and I turned and walked away. I left them to fend for themselves. It took less than a week before he sent for me."

"Now this man was pure evil, as the devil himself and he killed my Father and so many more slaves, he had to pay. He never knew his child educated me and the rest I learned right there, in his library. So after another week of eating cold slop, bed sores and his crazy wife eating bugs and her own feces, he broke, but not without conditions!" Nana said.

***

When Nana and Judith opened the door to the run-down slave house the stench made them lose their breakfast. This evil French bastard was getting The Learning from his slave woman and he didn't even know it.

Mr. Montague had been locked up with his Mrs. for only a week and it was enough!

"Weak children, I tell you slavery made them weak and us strong. They could not survive the hell they put us through. I told Mr. Montague to speak his terms, but he didn't notice Judith was writing them down as he spoke." Nana said.

"First, this land will always be Montague. You must go by Nana Montague, as well as, all your children. And most importantly, there must always be one Montague living on this plantation, until death and then replaced by another Montague," Mr. Montague snarled.

"So children one or more of you must decide who will stay before I'm gone. We have been thru too much to lose this place! Understood?" she asked.

"Yes, Nana," They replied.

"Second, he said he wanted fifty dollars for the property in its rundown state. Now remember we had forty dollars and I wasn't about to give him that. He must have been crazy as hell. I mean, just because his life dreams were destroyed and laying in rubble. Well, let's just say he wasn't going to stand in the way of my dreams. You know some people have no kind of vision. They can't see anything but trash when we see a rebirth. Now his third demand was that I take care of him and his wife until death."

"Well children, that didn't take too long. I agreed to all of his terms except the price. When I reminded him of how he killed my Father and made us all watch, he laughed and said he had to teach all the Niggas to fear him because he was closer to God. He was a white man."

"I immediately reminded him how my Father destroyed the trees and what he had, I have. Montague's face went stone as I spoke those words."

"Yeah I said if he was so close to God then he should heal himself and his land and his crazy ass wife. Furthermore, I'm an African and he and his people are the Niggas. Because only Niggas would treat humans as they did." Nana said with a chuckle.

"And with that, Judith and I left him and his wife to rot in their filthy tomb of a slave house."

***

Mrs. Montague was still babbling, "We are the Nigga slaves and Nana is the Master. The Master is going to get you. Be a good Nigga and do what the Master tells you to," as she laughed like the maniac she was.

Mr. Montague was sitting on the rundown

front porch when he stopped a boy child.

"Hey boy, go get that Nigga Gal Nana. I want to speak to her," he said.

Nana and Judith received the message and were headed to the slave house, to Montague.

"Judith, I'm not gonna be too many more Niggas, but if it's a Nigga Gal he wants, it's one he's gonna get," Nana said.

Judith was smiling because this is what she had been waiting for.

Montague was yelling at Nana as she walked up to him, "**I want some decent food and I need to bathe. Send that crazy bitch away from me before I lose my mind!**" He screamed.

"Ok, but you know what I want," Nana said.

"Do you agree to my terms?" he asked.

"All but one," said Nana.

"I'll give you thirty dollars for this beat down property; it's not even fit for a slave." She said.

Nana had pissed Montague off, and how dare a slave girl try to bargain with him.

"Fifty dollars and I'm tired of talking to you Nigga Gal, now do ..." he said as she cut him off.

Before he could finish his sentence, Nana's eyes caught his attention. Just like her Father's did that night...those eyes flushed him with fear. *Mentally* she raised him from a sitting position to standing on his one leg.

"Thirty dollars and your pathetic life depends on it," Nana said.

Montague was paralyzed with fear. He knew she was a witch and her voodoo was strong. He couldn't kill her like he did her Father but she could kill him or worst. She would let him live like a slave the rest of his life. Now he had upset Nana and she had nothing to lose!

"Do we have a deal, Montague?" Nana asked

"Put me down you witch!" he yelled.

Then his heart slowed down and he could hear it. He knew Nana was the cause as she turned her head slowly from side to side. It was like tick tock, you're running out of time.

"Do not vex me Montague; I will bury you alive, where no one will find you, you and your crazy wife. I'll bury the both of you alive, one on top of the other." She said.

"Stop, no, Gal stop!" He yelled as he fell down to a miserable filthy pile of flesh.

"Thirty dollars and not a penny less. You're too dumb to know it's not even worth it. You'll never outsmart me, Gal!" he yelled at Nana.

***

Nana sent a messenger for the Constable. His services were needed, and the next morning Nana had arranged a table and two chairs in the orchard. The Constable came in on a horse and was led to the table where Montague was seated and Nana was standing.

Montague had the papers in front of him:

"Good afternoon Mr. Montague," the Constable said. "I was told you needed me for official business."

"That's right Constable; as you can see my plantation is destroyed, as well as me, damn Northerners. I am bequeathing this property to my slave Gal Nana. She has been loyal to me and my wife and because this place is in ruins, it is not good enough for decent white folks, only a filthy slave." Montague said.

The Constable was sitting and reading the terms, "I see thirty dollars. Mr. Montague this place isn't worth ten dollars, no big house, just slave houses and run down fields, and now the slaves are free." He said.

"I still have to make the Niggas pay. They must pay their Masters and pay them well." Montague said.

"Can she read and write?" The Constable asked.

Montague laughed, "They don't have brains, that's why we do all the thinking, reading, and writing."

"Of course, she can't…well did you tell her the terms?" the Constable asked.

"Yes, what she needs to know," Montague said.

"Sign here Mr. Montague. Gal give your Master the money he is due and consider this a good deal for a Nigga like you." The Constable said.

Montague signed the deed and Nana gave him the money.

"Is it all there?" The Constable asked.

"Ooh yes!" Montague said as he observed the thirty dollars as if it were millions.

The Constable applied his official seal and signed his name.

"Gal, make your mark here," The Constable said.

Nana took the quill and dipped it into the ink and slid the excess on the tip of the inkwell. As both men watched in amazement, Nana signed her name in beautiful cursive letters: *Nana Montague*

The Constable looked at her and she smiled as he shook his head in disbelief.

He threw the deed towards her, shook Mr. Montague's hand and mounted his horse and left.

***

"That was a victorious day, children. From that day on, we owned this land and we worked for ourselves. Two of the terms have been met. Thirty dollars for the plantation and I took care of Mr. and Mrs. Montague until their deaths. They only lasted three years on slave food, in slave conditions. Now you know **I took my thirty dollars back**! And DW, my son the attorney, made sure thru the years that my deed is locked solid. I don't trust white people when it comes to African affairs," They all laughed.

"Oh and I exhumed Karen's remains and took all of their dead bodies to the end of the property and buried them outside the property line. Since then, the cemetery is filled with our people."

"Finally, the first term…one of you will have to live here for the rest of his/her life. Think now children don't wait. Understand?" Nana asked.

As they all nodded their heads, Kip asked Nana, "just how did you get this plantation to this beautiful state?"

"Remember I asked everyone to stay. Well child, word got out to all the slaves in the vicinity and before I knew it, we were housing the most skilled Masters of their crafts. We had Master builders, masons, artist, musicians, cooks, seamstress, laundry ladies, midwives, farmers, hunters, fishermen, blacksmith."

"Child, we had the best horse trainers and breeders, they all came here. I offered them land to build their homes and they never had to leave. They had food for their work and harvest to sell, livestock to raise and sell and nourish them. Most importantly, they could live, love and be a family as it was meant to be."

"The men could finally be the head of the household, have a purpose, provide and protect their families. We respected them and that made them proud. If they needed protection, I had my gift." Nana said.

"Within two years, the land produced a harvest. We had grass-fed livestock and we were selling clothing, as well as, doing laundry. We were strong, smart and skilled. White people were lazy and arrogant and dependent on us. But now we provided materials and services and they had to pay us for our work." She said.

They all smiled at Nana's victories.

"Now children don't think those white folks were happy for us, and the Klu Klux Klan came around here once. But bae-bae, Nana did some things and they didn't want any more of us."

"They spread it all around Louisiana that I was a voodoo witch…but our people knew better and it did the trick. I believe in an eye for an eye. If they burned anything here, I burned something of theirs at the identical time. If they killed our animals, then I killed theirs. Kill one of us and I killed one of them. Everything they did to us, I did to them. It didn't take but one visit and that shit stopped. You gotta fight fire with fire honey!" Nana said with a smile.

"Children we had parties, dinners and told African stories. We lived, loved and we were FREE, truly Free! To tell you the truth, I had no reason to leave here; this is my home." Nana said with a smile.

"However, I wanted a better life for my children. I insisted when they were of age, they joined friends that had gone up North for a better life."

"I had the money to send them to the finest African American Colleges, and they became skilled business owners. They are very successful in what they have chosen. Your Mothers and Fathers did that and I'm so proud of all my children. All of y'all make Nana so proud." She said.

"Twice a year your parents, my children, come home. They bring tools, workers and harvest the land and the livestock. We have one of the biggest contracts in the South for our vegetables and meat, as well as, the oil we sell from this land since 1960. As a matter of fact, my sons built this mansion for me and it has no reminisce of slavery."

"They insisted on giving me every modern appliance and the most current technology that I could ever want. This is our family home!"

"I don't know why Africans don't stick together anymore. We couldn't have made it without each other. We are survivors, smart and skilled. Don't ever forget your Learning. Be proud of your history and take care of each other and always thank SI, for he is God, an Amazing God!" Nana said in conclusion.

Nana had finished The Learning for the day and they all hugged and kiss each other. They took Nana back into the house because in four hours it would be dusk and time to lay Father to rest.

***

CHAPTER 5 Going Home

Several years ago Nana's sons had built a huge concrete crypt for this day. They built it into the land, on a hill, because Louisiana was below sea level. It was built with white concrete bricks, black cast iron doors; two white gaslight pillars flanked the front, one on the left and the other on the right. Two white cement flower pots were at the left and right of the doors; both were filled with African Violets.

Most importantly, Father's African sir name was engraved above the door in black letters and it read: **Bouso**.

All the other descendants of the estate occupied the white concrete above-ground caskets that surrounded the crypt and formed the African graveyard.

***

They were all dressed in white. Nana, Sissy, Judith, and Ty wore white headdresses. And as they walked to the barn, all their eyes were glowing gray, and the door opened on its own. Kip and Dennis had been there earlier to dress Father in all white linen and he lay there so peaceful ready to be laid to rest.

Without touch, they lifted him, Sissy and Ty in the front, one on the left and the other on the right.

Dennis and Kip were at his feet in the same formation, and Nana and Judith led the way. It was a slow honorable walk to the head of the cemetery. And as they got closer to the crypt, they could see the doors were already open, and the amber glow from the gas lights made it warm but very sad. It was precisely sunset when they entered.

There were eight concrete white caskets on the floor and empty slots on all three walls for other family members. Steven and Ty's mothers occupied two of the slots and it immediately came to Ty's mind the minute she walked through the doors.

Father's casket was adorned with Judith's handmade white linens and a white silk pillow. Gently, they laid his body into the casket and their eyes stopped glowing and soften to their beautiful natural state. Then everyone turned and looked at Nana.

Nana started weeping and struggled to speak her words. "Children bow your heads. Almighty SI we come to ask you for the forgiveness of our sins, especially the sins that provoke us to do bad. SI, please keep the family strong and embrace us with your love. SI, we especially ask you to take unto your fold the soul of Kimtu Bouso. SI, you gave us life and love. Unfortunately, Kimtu didn't have much of that here. SI, we lay him to rest until you awaken him into your leadership. Help us all to endure until that day, Amen."

"Amen!" All of them said in total agreement.

"Father I love you beyond death. May you rest in peace until SI's calling," Nana said and then she kissed his forehead. As she stepped back, her tears began to fall. One by one they said their goodbyes and kissed him, including Judith.

When they were done they stood in tears and Ty spoke, "thank you my Great, Grandfather without you, we would not be. We will carry on for you and pass on The Learning to the next generation. We will never forget our family's history." She said.

"Kimtu sleep, until we meet again," Kip said.

All their eyes shined the brightest white light as he laid there, a Beautiful Bamileke African Warrior.

The concrete lid lifted on its own and slowly moved into place until it covered him. And in the center of the white concrete lid in black letters it read: **Kimtu Bouso, SI, forget me not!**

As their eyes continued shining brightly, the lid on the second white casket to the right of him slid open, slowly revealing its emptiness.

"Yes, Mother Nettie you're next. Children, next we bring my Mother home to rest. Momma, we're coming to get you," Nana said.

***

CHAPTER 6 - I'm staying

Nana had a peaceful rest and was awakened to Sissy and Ty delivering breakfast trays to everyone's room.

"Good morning Nana, did you sleep well?" Sissy asked.

Nana was smiling when she said, "yes children, I slept in peace. I didn't dream, didn't worry, I just rested."

"Do we have The Learning today? Learning about Mother Nettie?" Sissy asked.

"Every day we have The Learning, child," Nana said.

"Nana I was hoping to go to the stable and ride one of the horses," Ty said.

"Child you love those horses and dogs. As a matter of fact, those two dogs been playing and running around like they just been freed," Nana said as they all laughed.

"Ever since you gave me those two; they have been my loyal, spoiled babies. I know if anyone tried to harm me, well those two…," as Nana cut Ty off.

"Ty those dogs' bloodline is almost as long as mine. Montague gave Karen the Mother dog as a pet.

She didn't like Karen, she liked me and I took care of her. So when her pups were born I always kept two and bred them strong. I gave you the last of the breeding. Those two boys you will breed and always keep two. They will be loyal for life." Nana said.

"Wow, Nana I didn't know that, but I will do just as you say," Ty said.

"You always have. Anyway child, we'll start The Learning after dinner. So today you children get familiar with this place because it's going to be home for one of you." Nana said.

"Ok Nana," they concluded.

"Oh Nana, we love you!" they said.

"I love you all, with all my heart," Nana said as she continued sipping her coffee and looking out her window at the beautiful day. Nana loves her coffee!

Sissy and Ty finished the breakfast deliveries and then they both went into Sissy's room for some real woman talk.

***

"Now that you've got me here, I assume you need to talk personal," said Sissy.

"Yeah Cuz, first I called my realtor and all my employees. Of course, you know about Luis's cheating ass. I knew. I was just hoping he would confess, repent and get over his midlife crisis. Hell, he could have told me the truth and left." Ty said.

"So I had to drop the bomb on him and get it off my chest. Wow, it felt good to see him scared to death of what I could do to him!" Ty said sarcastic as hell, as they both laughed.

"Oh, that was good entertainment. But I know you loved him, Ty." Sissy said.

"Yeah, but I love me more! Cuz you gotta know your self-worth, and the fact that I was good to his ass, I deserve a man that will be good to me. This shit makes me never want to be in a relationship again." Ty said.

"Now the realtor?" Sissy asked.

"Yep, I'm selling my house. It shouldn't take long. A four bedroom brick ranch with an in-ground pool in Florida, SOLD!" Ty said.

"Ty, where are you going with this clean slate?" Sissy asked.

"I'm staying! I am Nana's replacement. The decision came to me fast and easy. I'm single and I don't want to be married. I have spent a lot of time right here with Nana, growing up. Basically, I can do what I want and make all decisions concerning me." Ty said.

"Yes you are headstrong and you are your own boss. I'm not surprised. If I had to pick it would be you. You get it; you know that money is just to do the things necessary to keep this place running and to help the family, not to be worshiped. Besides, you have your own cash. You have the compassion to care for others and you made the promise to our Great, Grandfather to pass on The Learning." Sissy said.

Ty couldn't contain her smile, "I knew you would understand and I'm moving my company here and as many of my personnel as I can. I'm going to look at commercial property. Then I'm going to buy some land and develop a subdivision of houses. I want to offer my people free housing as an incentive to make that move. I know I can do this." She said.

"I called my assistant and told her to send my personal furniture and everything in my office."

"The rest I'll give to charity, I'll write it off to expenses. Within two weeks it's should be a wrap. But I have to ask Nana about building a plane hangar, landing strip, and a helipad, so I can be mobile when I need to be." Ty said.

"Ty you know Nana will let you do whatever you need to. That's Nana, a woman with a vision and always ahead of her time." Sissy added.

"You ain't never lied. Especially how she told us she had a vision and a plan to own this place. Nana is…The Shit!" Ty said.

"No doubt about it…The Shit!" Sissy repeated.

"I'll let the others know." Ty said.

"Ty you're not the least bit scared to stay in this mansion with all this land and two dogs?" Sissy asked.

"Sissy those two dogs will defend me to the death. And need you forget our gift; I can link you guys from anywhere, anytime I need to. As for me, my mind is made up!" Ty said.

"So let it be written, so let it be done!" Sissy said like the Pharaoh in the Ten Commandments.

"Sissy I have a feeling our ancestors protect us way past death." Ty said.

"Funny I have that same feeling. It's a good thing we're not scary." Sissy said.

"It's the damnedest thing, with the way the world is today, Nana has lived here all this time. Even after her children left and everyone else either left or died. She and Judith, uneventfully live here. Sissy, I tell you there is something unsaid and Nana has got to tell us everything." Ty said.

"I'm thinking the same thing. You know Ty; I

think this gift is much more than she told us." Sissy said.

***

Dennis and Kip were standing outside by the cars talking.

"Dennis, man if I had a three-wheeler," Kip said.

"Ooh hell yeah...this is a good riding day," said Dennis.

"We got money, SI is good and why don't we get Sissy and Ty and head out to the Harley Davidson dealership?" Kip asked.

"Sissy?" Dennis asked *mentally*.

"What do you want?" Sissy said sarcastic as hell.

"Money, what else? No, no just joking Sis. Listen, Kip and I are going into town to get some three-wheelers. You and Ty want to come with?" Dennis asked.

"Ooh yeah let's do this, see you in five," Sissy replied.

"They're on the way and down with the plan," Dennis said to Kip.

"Remember how we taught those two how to ride. Sissy is a straight up Tomboy and Ty is a Wild Card," Kip said.

"Yeah Sissy might be a Tomboy and Ty a Wild Card, but they're two of the finest females in all of Louisiana," Dennis said as him and Kip laughed loudly.

***

They all went in one car as they headed to the Harley Davidson Dealership.

"Listen ladies, here's the scoop. We get a package deal, four three-wheel motorcycles at one base price. Let me take care of the negotiations. New Yorkers can wheel and deal, believe that. I figure we'll buy them and store them here. So when we come back we can ride as much as we want." Kip said with authority.

"Well you better ask Ty about that, she's staying. Ha-ha little Nana is the next heir of the Montague Plantation," Sissy informed them.

"No shit!" they said in unison.

"No shit!" Ty said in confirmation.

"You're the perfect fit. A wild card; just like Nana. Um, excuse me Ma'am; may we store the bikes at your place of residence?" Kip asked.

"You most certainly may." Ty said.

All of them were laughing and calling Ty little

Nana as they pulled up to the dealership. As they exited the car, they all hovered around the three-wheelers. Ty mounted the Red Tri Glide, Dennis the Black one, Sissy the White and Kip the Midnight Blue.

"Are we good?" Ty asked everyone.

"Oh we good," as it was unanimous.

Kip and Ty filled out the paperwork and were just about to complete the wire transfer for a smooth one hundred thirty thousand dollars when Ty spotted the Gear Shop.

"Oh, we forgot to tell you, this deal includes four full sets of gear, right?" Ty asked the overzealous salesman.

"Well Ma'am, I'll have to clear it with my manager," he said.

"You tell your manager if it doesn't, we have

three days to cancel this contract and easy come, easy go." Ty said.

As the Manager entered the room he went straight to Kip.

"Mr. Montague can we work this deal out?" he asked.

Ty stood up to oppose his assumption.

"It's Ms. Montague and he's not my husband, he's my cousin. I'm the one calling the shots. Either we have a complete deal or you just lost one hundred thirty thousand dollars. I want full gear for four people to go along with the bikes. Yes, or No, speak now." Ty said.

"Yes, Ma'am we have a deal and thank you so much for buying at Henrick's Harley Davidson." The manager said.

Ty flashed him a quick bright gray wink.

"Did I tell you what a pleasure it is? Thank you and would you personally see to the final inspection of our bikes?" Ty asked.

"Yes Ma'am, I most certainly will." he said as he ran to handle Ty's request.

"Little Nana all the way," Kip said.

***

Nana and Judith were sitting on the front porch. Nana was enjoying a good puff on her pipe when Judith stood up. Nana's eyes were gazing on them. Sissy and Ty were in front riding side by side. Dennis was on the other side of Sissy, behind her, and Kip was on the other side of Ty, behind her.

They were dressed in black leather, leather chaps, leather jackets, leather gloves, boots and their helmets were color matched to their bikes. Their faces were covered with the dark tinted safety shields, looking like the Zulus as they pulled up to the front porch.

"Nana look at your children, they are too much, just too much!" Judith Squealed.

Nana stood up and smiled as they turned the bikes off and raised their safety shields from their faces.

"Nana, Ms. Judith you like?" They asked.

"I love it. What kind of riding machine is this?" Judith asked as she and Nana stepped down to examine them and the bikes.

"This is where you're gonna sit," Kip said to Judith.

"Ooh no, not me Kip," Judith begrudgingly stated.

"Ooh yes, you," Kip said.

"Well, where am I gonna sit?" Nana asked.

"Right here behind me." Ty said.

"Dennis help Nana get up here and put on this helmet and seat belt her in," Ty commanded.

Kip was putting Judith in the back seat, helmet on and safety belt too.

"Ladies you're gonna love this," Kip said.

"Kip, ride to my right and Dennis and Sissy follow us." Ty ordered.

"Ok little Nana," They said in union.

"Why they call you little me?" Nana asked between her laughter.

"Because, I have decided to stay!" Ty replied.

"Ooh I knew that baby," Nana said with a smile.

***

It was a clear, beautiful blue sky day and they knew Nana and Judith had never ridden on bikes.

They drove smoothly as they witness the beauty of the Montague estate.

Nana's children had rebuilt the houses the free slave made. All the houses were to the right behind the mansion. They named the houses after the families that lived in them and each had a plague that told the story of their lives.

Behind the houses were the stables and the barn that housed the horses, and the other livestock. Everyone knew Nana's animal where grass feed and her harvest was organic, pesticide never touched them. Africans knew how to fight insects with other insects. All natural cared for and originally sewn by the master farmers that lived here.

Next to the stables and the barn were the orchards and the massive gardens. They took their time riding through the pear and apple trees.

Just the smell of them was heavenly. There were pecan trees and even grape vines, dark red and light green grapes. Nana knew how to make wine out of every fruit and some vegetables, and Ty planned on learning from her.

To the left of the mansion was where Ty was hoping to place a plane hangar, landing strip and a helipad. Beautiful acres of green land were just perfect for that purpose.

The Montagues had no neighbors, just open land for as far as you can see. They rode to the full depth of the plantation and saw the huge pond for the fishery and crawfishing. You could literally place four NFL stadiums side by side on this land and still, have room. It made the children proud to see the beauty of this place.

As they circled around to the front, on the left

side of the mansion; three-fourths of a mile up was the massive African graveyard.

In front of it was an enormous flower bed full of red, yellow and white roses. Roses were Nana's favorite flower and they were set in a huge circle with the letter "M" in the middle.

The "M" was designed with the red roses at the tips of it, and the yellow in the middle with white roses at the ends. It had an ombre effect.

Old trees cocooned the red brick driveway to the mansion, and to the right of the driveway was a white gazebo flank with perfectly trimmed berry bushes. There were white cast iron benches and chairs. It looked like a place to have a concert in the park.

Finally, at the very front entrance of the property is the ten-foot white brick gate, with the black cast iron doors. On the left and the right of the gate are two huge three tier, white fountains.

***

They sat at the top of the long driveway to the mansion. Ty turned off her engine and the rest of them followed her lead.

"Nana, this is so beautiful," Ty stated.

Nana spoke as she raised the shield from her face, "You children breathe new life into her, into me. Ty I trust you and I know you will keep your promise to Father. You are little me," and they all laughed as Ty laughed and a tear fell from her eye as she looked at her home and smiled.

***

With the motorcycles parked in the circular driveway, Nana, Judith, and all the children were sitting, relaxing and laughing.

"Ms. Judith and Nana, you're riders now. There is nothing like riding on this beautiful land, taking in the fresh air and the beautiful sunshine." Kip said.

"I have never had so much fun. I never knew these motorcycles things existed. I like it." Ms. Judith said in pure excitement.

"I told you Judith, these children breathe new life, new hope and a new day into this old land and this old lady. It's been a long time since I have seen all of this property. It's too big for me to walk it but it is just as I remembered, Home! I've never been a slave, children. No one can enslave your mind unless you let them. I've always been free!" Nana said.

"Nana me too, I play by my own rules. I do what I want, when I want and how I want." Ty stated.

"Wild cards you two, never can predict what you will do next. Both of you are free spirits." Kip said.

"That's why I knew Ty would stay. Sissy is made for a husband and children. Dennis is close to his Father and that's a good thing because only a real man can teach you to be a man. Kip, you're non-committal and you don't know why. Later in life, you'll find out. But this only child, she doesn't mind her solitude and peace of mind. She creates better when she is alone. Her vision is like mine, creative, headstrong and believes in SI with all her heart. So tomorrow I'll call my Son DW and deed this place over to you and your Cousin. I know in my heart it is the right thing to do." Nana said.

"Nana I love you so much. It will be my honor to care for all that you have sacrificed for."

"Thank you for trusting me too, but are you talking about the other third generation, first and only child, the man?" Ty asked.

"Yes Ty, he has reached the same decision you have. He is perfect to be the head of the household and you two will complement each other well. He is the yang to your yin. So that's it, it's done!" Nana said.

"Well, now that's decided, it's time for me to go in here and start dinner," Judith said.

"Ms. Judith you take a break. Ty and I will cook dinner. Just relax," said Sissy.

"Ooh, that's so nice of you babies," Judith said.

"It's our pleasure." They said.

"After dinner children, we have The Learning," Nana stated.

***

Ty and Sissy went inside to cook and Ms. Judith and Nana rocked, and talked as they watched Kip and Dennis wash and wipe down the bikes before putting them away.

"Dinner is served!" Sissy announced.

They had cooked smothered pork chops in gravy, over rice and snap green beans with skillet corn and homemade yeast rolls. For dessert, they had baked apple pies and served them with a big scoop of homemade vanilla ice cream.

The family finished up dinner and Ty and Sissy cleared the table while Nana, Judith, Kip, and Dennis went to the great room. After doing the dishes and cleaning up, Sissy and Ty joined them.

"Nana you want the book?" Dennis asked.

"Yes child, and this time Judith stays with us," Nana said.

***

CHAPTER 7 – *Mother Nettie*

All were seated around Nana as she opened the book and started to read:

"Mother Nettie was bought by Montague two years before he bought my Father. She was seventeen years old. Mother was kidnapped from Africa the same as my Father, different tribe, same hell, same struggle, but she was a woman-child."

"She avoided being raped during the journey and here on the plantation, that was unusual for a woman. The Montagues sent her to the big house to be trained in cooking and cleaning under the dictatorship of Mrs. Montague."

"Now when Montague bought Father, he had decided to mate him with Nettie to make strong slaves that he didn't have to pay for. Slave owners felt any child born on their property belonged to them." Nana said.

"Nettie took one look at Father and considered herself blessed. You see children, Nettie was maybe five feet tall and Sissy you are built like her. Both of you have big breast, small waist, and child bearing hips. Compact but strong." Nana and Sissy smiled.

"She was very attractive, pretty with the color of sweet caramel."

"Just like me, just like all the women in our family and every one of us has thick hair with a loose curl."

"Sissy it's no surprise that you are a Registered Nurse and specialize in Trauma Care. Mother Nettie was a healer in her land just like her Mother before her." Nana said as Sissy smiled the brightest.

"Well, I guess Father was smitten too. He was always holding her hand and she was always willing to go where he went. She said she would follow him back to Africa. Her home was with him. She even wanted to die with him. That's what kind of love they had. You know, that was Father's plan."

"He and Nettie had a secret African wedding. And unknowing to Mr. Montague, Father was not siring dogs; he was planning his family with his wife. They never mated; they made love the way SI meant it to be. Mother was proud and so was Father. They were husband and wife under one accord with SI. Until that day, the day Montague killed Father. And on that day, Nettie died too, she died inside." Nana said as she shook her head and her face was riddled with the scars of the memory.

"Dear God, if Montague wouldn't let him be free then SI freed him through death," Nana said.

***

The children did not like to see Nana cry or be upset, it angered them. It also angered them as to how their ancestors had been treated. Something inside of them and Nana demanded justice! And SI help anyone that would cause any harm or suffering to Nana. They were the new generation, and they had decided no more would their family be unprotected or subject to this bullshit.

Just try them. All their eyes blazed white when they looked at each other as they all *mentally* heard themselves say, "don't fuck with us and ours! Just try it, so help us SI."

Venom filled their gray-white eyes and it didn't go unnoticed by Nana and Judith. Nana did her best to compose herself to continue, as heart-wrenching as it was, it had to be completed.

***

"The day after my Father's death, Mother did not speak and never would speak again. Her dreams died in that river with him. Montague said she was useless and anything he deemed useless was only of value if he could sell it." Nana said.

"It was exactly two months after Father was murdered, Mother was sold. I didn't know where she was, only that her fate was going to be that of

Father's. It was as if she wanted it that way. If she couldn't be with him in living, then she would be with him in death."

"When the free slaves came here to live, some of them knew of my Mother and her fate. They told me she was sold to the Franklin Plantation. The Franklin Plantation was owned by the two Franklin sisters. They were two of the most hated, evil, ugly white women that ever lived in Louisiana." She said.

"Justine Franklin's husband and only Son had died in a fire that burned down their barns, and the back half of the Big House. It happened when the civil war was starting, and they could never rebuild it because their slaves were fleeing and some of them came here. So the place was falling apart. And when the Northern Soldiers came, well they just finished it."

"Now Justine's younger sister, Ernestine Franklin, came to stay with her. She was a bitter, cynical, spinster. She was as tall as an amazon with the personality of an ogre." Nana said.

"They had bought Mother to work as a personal maid and to help out in the fields. Mother went from one hell to another. Even after the beatings, she never complied."

"This made Ernestine Franklin grow more and more frustrated, and in a fit of anger, she hit Mother with a cast iron skillet, in her head. My Mother died lying on the kitchen floor with half her brains spewing out of her skull." Nana gasped and then she pushed the words out: **"Freed by SI thru death!"** Nana cried.

Judith was rubbing Nana's back as she lowered her head and shook it from side to side at the disbelief of how inhumane they were treated. The children's eyes had lit up the room. It was sheer anger, compounded with the murders of Nettie and Kimtu.

Dennis screamed out his words and paced the floor with uncontrolled fury:

"**AW, Hell NO!** I say we dig their dead asses up and burn what's left of them. **No, No Kip**; you know this shit goes beyond saying. **Never, and I mean, Never again.**" He yelled.

Dennis left out the front door holding his head as if he was holding on to his sanity.

"No children, let him go. I know his anger and his pain. There were times when I thought I would lose my mind too. All the murdering, raping, and whippings. It was a nightmare I thought would never end."

"Even after being freed, the Klu Klux Klan with their terrorizing and hangings, but they didn't scare me and I would never be intimidated by cowards hiding behind sheets and full of liquid courage." Nana said.

"I'm angry too Nana, but I'm hurt that our people were treated worse than animals and not too much has changed today. You have your corporate Uncle Tom's, selling their soul to the corporations for a title and money, acting like slave overseers."

"There are **some** black men who are brainwashed to believe if they get a white woman, a Mercedes, and simulate whiteness then they are more acceptable to society. Oh and they want their children born with good hair and fair skin. "She's not black, she's bi-racial." Then why she need black hair products for her bi-racial hair. Get her ass some VO5 and see how that works out for you!"

"Oh Jesus, can you believe all of this, just because they have been taught their blackness is inferior. So now they are still conditioned mentally to act just like a house nigga."

"This shit started right here on these plantations. When the weak believed if they found favor with the Master they would be better than the ones in the fields. Misplaced loyalty and they couldn't see that they were still enslaved; in the field or the big house, they were still slaves! The mental damage is still here today." Sissy said with total disgust.

"Sissy speaks the truth, Nana. They tried to destroy our families, and for the most part they did a good job of it. If you destroy the integrity of the man then the woman will go on without him."

"They depicted our men as lazy, ignorant, thieves, murders, rapist, all out criminals and thugs. It was in the media, the cartoons, in the movies. And today, it's still being done."

"I absolutely hate television. It is one big propaganda to show that white is superior. We are bombarded with advertisements that depict the white woman as the epitome of beauty. If you do see a sister on television, she is mixed or advertising cleaning products. Cleaning products, really, like a house maid. Only our commercials and channels show our dark beautiful sisters as beautiful women too. The truth is we come in every shade and all of us are beautiful!"

"This divide and conquer is not working for me. We give birth to the black man. We go through the same struggle, maybe worse."

"We have been told we are not beautiful with our big lips, big hips, and our brown skin. Now everywhere you look big lips, big butts, and tans. Why would you desire to be what you hate so much?"

"Have you notice that 99.9 percent of movies feature the white man as the hero or the lead in the movie. There is very little being shown that uplifts our men. And I can't even begin to go in on those ignorant housewives shows. The sisters I know are not ignorant, loud mouth, bitchy and whorish. They are too busy working to keep a roof over their head and food in their children's mouths."

"Yes I'm pissed off too, but there is just one more thing. It's seldom told that most Rappers and Entertainers are college educated and business orientated. Or if your bank account looks like B and J's you have to be involved in the Illuminati."

"Is it just possible that they have earned every dime of it? But then again, who is really buying the music? Stealing our culture, our music, the way we speak? **WHO?**"

"When will our people wake the hell up? It was all a brainwash to get a race of people enslaved, physically and mentally. We are all humans and until every generation of racist dies off, this shit will go on and on."

"I swear Nana, I try to control my feelings but sometimes I just want to let go and…." Ty stopped.

"Child what?" Nana asked.

"GO STRAIGHT AFRICAN WARRIOR ON THEIR ASSES!" Ty yelled.

Nana's face went from serious to a burst of laughter. Judith got a case of the giggles and Kip, Sissy and Ty released and let themselves laugh too.

Just then Dennis came back in the house; his face was twisted with confusion.

"I don't know what's so funny, but I could really use a joke right now," Dennis said.

"Are you alright little brother? I know it's hard but you need to get a grip because I have a feeling things get worse before they get better." Kip said.

"Nana, I'm so sorry, but I…" Dennis said.

"Child I know, believe me I know. We gotta get through this children; because once you know, don't you ever forget your Learning!" Nana said.

"Nana, you and Ms. Judith lived this and that makes me admire and respect both of you, even more. Just know there is nothing we wouldn't do for the both of you!" Kip said.

Everyone stood up and kissed and hugged Nana and Judith and set back down because The

Learning was not over.

"Children the slaves buried Mother in the slave graveyard on the Franklin property. Now believe me when I say evil lives a long time! Even though Justine died twenty years ago; Ernestine Franklin is still alive and living on what remains of The Franklin Plantation where Mother is buried."

"I know you all know that if you do what was done to you, that makes you no better than those that have persecuted you and yours. We are a proud and responsible people, but if nice don't work..."

Kip finished Nana's sentence, "we take what is ours." He said.

"Sorry to say, but yes, we take what is ours. Then tomorrow we leave out early because the Franklin Plantation is thirty miles south of us, close to New Orleans." Nana said.

"I must warn you, unlike Father, Mother was laid in the ground and not in a casket. Louisiana is below sea level, so I'm pretty sure there is no flesh left. But we know our bloodline down to the bone marrow, and tomorrow we bring Mother home." Nana said.

"Nana I know you're tired and it's getting late but, I really want to know how Ms. Judith is related to us? I mean we see the resemblance. So…" Dennis asked.

"I'm Judith Montague, ninth child and the last of Father Kimtu and Mother Nettie's children," Judith stated.

Nana had a chuckle in her voice because it was so unlike Judith to be forward.

"Judith is my baby sister. Montague thought she was slow and that she is not. She is smart, outsmarted him. Judith reads, writes and loves music and cooking."

"She takes care of me, like I took care of her when Montague wanted to sell her. I convinced him if he left her to my care she would be alright, and she was. Don't think because she's quiet that she is slow. Judith is more of a delicate flower than I am." Nana said.

"This is Judith's home. Say no more Nana. Ms. Judith, you are blood and anything you want or need, I got you for life." Ty said with conviction.

"We're family and we always take care of our own. Now Mr. Dennis, are you satisfied?" Nana asked.

"Aww Nana, now we can spoil Ms. Judith like we spoil you," he said.

Everyone smiled and laughed.

"Well children, let's call it a night."

"That's enough of The Learning for now," Nana said as they turned the lights off and everyone headed upstairs to bed.

***

Nana and Judith went to sleep first, but Dennis, Sissy, Kip, and Ty were wide awake in Sissy's bedroom, having a late night chat.

"Man, SI knows best. I would have been down with Great Grand Kimtu; they would have had to kill me too." Kip said.

"What makes you guys think anything has changed? I can turn on Cops and watch white people fight the police. They spit on them, resist arrest, try to speed away from them, and not one of them are ever shot or killed. That's right now and it's murder. Just like slavery days. They could take our lives and nothing was done to them."

"Well, I know one thing; I will not be sitting around singing we shall overcome," Ty said.

"And that goes double for me!" Kip stated.

"You know I can go zero to one hundred in a millisecond," Dennis said.

"I'm with the Wild Card," Sissy said.

"So this Ernestine Franklin..." Kip said as Dennis cut him off.

"I say we go and clobber that old Bitch," Dennis said without a smile.

Sissy was laughing hysterically, "this damn fool, and that makes us no better than her."

Ty said seriously and not cracking a smile, "Dennis for once I agree with you. She killed our Great Grandmother like some kind of animal. I can't forgive that. I say we go straight Ninja on her ass, up her ass, around her ass, or between her ass!"

"Do onto other as they have done onto you. An eye for an eye and that old Bitch owes us an eye!"

"Ok Sissy, Ty, and Dennis are straight trippin, but wait…maybe they have the right idea." Kip said, then he broke out laughing like a psycho, all of them did.

"Listen here: we are the new generation of Bamileke Warriors. We get the job done by any means necessary, and if necessary, we'll do you. So don't make it necessary. That's our Modus Operandi. Now analyze that because play time is over!" Ty said and they all concurred.

***

CHAPTER 8 - Almost home!

Nana and Judith were sound asleep when Kip, Ty, Sissy, and Dennis left for the Franklin plantation. The night before they had googled the necessary information to make the trip; but most importantly they had decided to do this on their own. Nana needed to sit this one out.

Because they knew, they would have to fight fire with fire to get Mother Nettie back.

***

They were one hour outside of New Orleans when they stopped at an Army Navy store for the supplies they needed. The children knew they had kin folks in New Orleans and one, in particular, they wanted to visit.

Uncle David, Nana's third child. All of them loved and respected Uncle David. He was the most outspoken and free-spirited of all Nana's children. Uncle David was fearless and that's just what they needed, a fearless, Wild Card Warrior.

It was forty-five minutes later when Kip pulled Ty's SUV into Uncle David's driveway. He heard them pull in and met them at the door.

Uncle David is a younger version of his Grandfather. He stands six foot, one inch tall, with skin the color of African soil, blue-black, long loose curls rest on his shoulders. He has a keen nose and lips a woman would die for with naturally arched eyebrows. His mustache and his beard are meticulously groomed, and of course, he has those piercing gray eyes.

***

Sissy and Ty left the vehicle first and went straight into his waiting arms.

"Uncle David, you look like a modern Kimtu. A fine specimen of a man," Sissy said.

"You're one of SI's finest, a seasoned Warrior!" Ty exclaimed.

David was standing there eating up the praises, "my two favorite nieces."

"You two sure know how to make an old man feel good." He said.

Uncle David embraced Sissy and Ty and their arms were wrapped around him as Dennis and Kip walked right into the fold.

They stood there for a while; it was quiet but not *mentally*. They could hear each other saying the words: "my family, we stand strong with SI. SI bless Nettie and Kimtu for our very existence."

"Well children, come on in we have much to discuss. First, does Momma know you're here?" David asked.

"Uncle David we left her a note telling her we were here in New Orleans, and we needed her to trust us on this one," Kip said.

"Now you know Momma will be watching." Uncle David said as all of them laughed because they knew that for sure.

"Uncle David like we told you last night, we are going to bring Mother Nettie home and it's not going to be easy," Dennis said.

"But children I had time to think about your plan. Of course, I love it but I need to tell you a little more about your gift."

"As for Steven my son, he has decided to join you and he will be staying with you, Ty. You won't be living at The Montague alone." Uncle David said.

"You know Steven is the third generation, first born Male, an only child. Yes, it's three of you first born. But, the male child has the DNA of Kimtu and that makes his gift stronger than the women. So with his female counterpart...well!" Uncle David said as he smiled at Ty.

Ty was holding Uncle David's hand and

remembering how she and Steven were really close. Steven stood taller than his Father and had the same skin tone, the same hair, just longer. He was a spitting image of his Father and Nana's Father, and of course, he has those gray eyes. Wow, our bloodline is very strong, Ty thought to herself.

"That's great news, I just love Steven. He's smooth and smart." Ty said.

"I have taught my son well, but Steven's gift is stronger than mine; as strong as Kip's. But his is more developed, after all, he is the eldest. Ty you and Steven are both the only child. So you must have..." Uncle David stopped his sentence as he looked down into her eyes and both sets of eyes blazed a strong gray light.

"Um yes, you do." Uncle David said.

"What is it, Uncle David?" Ty asked.

"The dreams...pay close attention to the ones that forecast danger; those are the ones that matter." Uncle David said.

"And Dennis," as Uncle David changed his stare to Dennis' eyes.

"Dennis, you just be careful. Don't follow thru on your thoughts. It's alright to be angry but vengeance belongs to SI. Don't be bitter and full of malice, it will consume you. Remember son, hate destroys the hater. So Dennis, change your direction. Please listen to me." He said.

Uncle David grabbed Dennis by the shoulders and hugged him hard. Everyone was focused on the words that were said: "Hate destroys the hater."

They were so focused on what Uncle David said that they didn't notice Steven Montague had entered the front door.

"Cousins," Steven said.

They all jump up with smiles, hugs, and kisses for Steven. Then they all sat in the living room with Uncle David at the head of them all.

"Ty I guess dad told you I'm coming to live at the Montague with you," Steven said.

"This is even better than I could have hoped. Steven, you are an architect like your Father?" Ty asked.

"Sure, and yes we have the blueprints to Nana's place," Steven said.

"You're reading my thoughts again. Then you know we need a landing strip, helipad, and a hangar." Ty said.

"Sure do and I've been working on the plans. Ty when we get home I need to show you some things about the Montague estate." Steven said.

"Now this is going to be interesting and I can't wait," Ty said.

"But first, Dad do you mind going over the plans with us for tonight?" Steven asked.

"Alright everybody, let's get to work." Uncle David said.

All of them were sitting in Uncle David's living room confirming what would be done and just how they were going to get it done.

After dinner, they left out. They were headed to the Franklin Plantation on one accord and with one single thought. Bring Mother Nettie home!

***

Nana, Judith and Uncle David were all *mentally* tuned in as Kip pulled the SUV up to the twisted and mangled gate of the Franklin Plantation. It took very little effort for them *mentally* to lift the broken gate. Without one creek, they lifted and opened one side, then entered the property and slowly and methodically closed it. With the lights off, Kip parked the SUV into an overgrown orchard, just far away from the gate as not to be seen by anyone passing by.

One by one they exited. They were dressed in all black fatigues, black boots, black gloves, black backpacks and a black ski mask that covered everything except their gray eyes. However, Sissy was dressed like a battered slave maid.

They all darted thru the trees as they instinctively headed deep on the property to the slave's graves.

"Mama would you look at them," David said *mentally*.

Nana couldn't help but chuckle as she replied, "Yes son, they look like a Swat Team."

"Or Black Ninjas," David laughed.

"Dad, Nana we can hear you," Steven said.

That just made Nana and David laugh even harder.

"Well go head on children!" Nana said.

It was an all-out struggle to bend down the overgrown foliage and make their way to what remained of the big house. All of them noticed their boots were sinking deep into the overgrown grass. Dennis stopped for a moment and surveyed the grounds. Immediately he knew why but the others were focused on getting to the slave graves.

The graves were generally located to the very back of the property and not marked. Dennis and Sissy were to stay near the big house, just in case...just then they all heard it, a pump shotgun being cocked!

"Who's there? I know I heard someone on

my property. I said who's there?" She said as she started making out the figure of an African slave girl.

Sissy was the girl she saw dressed in a maid's uniform. Ernestine lowered the barrel of the shotgun as she spoke thru shallow wheezes:

"Gal, what are you doing out there?" Ernestine said.

"Ms. Ernestine it's me, Nettie your maid. You remember me don't you?" Sissy asked.

Ernestine was searching her memory because there had been so many.

"Gal, what you say your name is?" Ernestine asked.

"Ms. Ernestine, I'm Nettie. Years ago you bought me from Mr. Montague to be your personal maid." Sissy said.

***

Steven, Kip, and Ty had to leave them to reach the graveyard. They could feel they were getting closer and then they saw it; a large Magnolia tree with decaying flowers littering the ground. They took off their backpacks and Ty's eyes were first to shine bright gray. She was standing on top of Mother Nettie's grave but something was wrong. Steven's eyes were shining bright gray too. Two family members were here.

"What the hell! I'm sure Mother Nettie is right here, but Steven…" Ty said.

"It's small Ty, but it's one of ours. It's a baby!" Steven said.

Nana gasped as her eyes went gray-white. She heard herself say, "A baby! Mother was pregnant with Father's last child!" She said.

"Ty step back and Steven stay there,"

Kip said.

Kip and Ty linked and the ground started to move away from Mother Nettie's remains. Kip removed the silk pillowcase from his backpack as Ty removed every bone. It took extra care for her to gather the skull. There was an open gash and the eye socket had a deep crack in it, one that ran the length of the back of her skull. Kip carefully placed the pillowcase into Ty's backpack and zipped it closed.

"Ok Steven, back up." said Kip.

Steven stepped back as they all linked and carefully removed the ground from the newborn. Kip didn't have another silk pillow case so he carefully removed every little bone from the grave and placed it into Steven's backpack.

"It was a boy, a stillborn," Steven said.

All of them took in a deep breath and headed

towards the big house, to the truck, but Sissy and Dennis had heard every word.

"She murdered Mother Nettie and she was pregnant. She owes us two eyes, Ty," Dennis said *mentally* and Ty heard him.

Now he was really tired of playing with this old Bitch's mind.

"Come on in here Gal. You got lots of work to do," Ernestine said.

Kip, Steven, and Ty had just made it to the big house and were standing next to Dennis watching Ernestine.

Ernestine walked into the house with the shot-gun by her side. "Nigga, I'm not gonna tell you again. Get your black ass in this house and get to cleaning. Don't make me shoot you." Ernestine said as she turned around to make her point clear.

Sissy went to talk but couldn't make a sound. Dennis had projected an image of her with her head protruding brains and blood gushing down her uniform. Ernestine saw a decomposing Nettie, a distorted neck, and her head leaned to the side of the wound with eyes blazing white. Dennis spoke as it appeared that Nettie was speaking.

"Do you know who I am now? I am Nettie, BITCH! I am the same Nettie that you killed with a cast iron skillet. I was with child when you killed me. I've come back for you, you evil, ugly, sinister, old BITCH!" Dennis yelled.

Ernestine immediately remembered what she had done. She remembered the day she killed Nettie and the baby left Nettie's body the moment she died.

She recalled how she ordered the slave women to remove Nettie's disgusting remains from her kitchen. It was then that she noticed all the white eyes coming from the darkness behind Nettie.

"**You Goddamn Niggas not gonna kill me!**" Ernestine screamed.

She was standing in the kitchen door when she raised the barrel of the shotgun and aimed it right at Sissy. Before she could fire, Dennis released all the hate and anger he had inside. **"Two eyes, you owe us Two!"** he said out loud and she heard him.

The house shook and the ground sucked it down so fast that Kip had to grab Sissy and run. Ty was behind them when Steven grabbed Dennis just in time. As the sinkhole widen, it continued to expand as they were running for their lives. But if things couldn't get worse, the ground beneath them was getting soggier and it became harder for them to lift their legs.

They were too far away from the SUV and the sinkhole was expanding the width of the property and quickly catching up to the length of it. Nana took Judith's hand and *mentally* told David and Judith to link with the children. Steven and Kip caught the link as soon as it was sent.

Everyone's eyes were blazing white light when it hit the SUV. Within seconds the SUV was lifted over the broken down gate and placed safely down the road away from the property. All the doors were opened and the engine was running, just waiting for them. As they got closer to the dilapidated gate the ground gave way. It sucked them down so quickly there was no time for them to think!

Instinctively, they reached out to each other, holding on tight as the water filled the whole plantation.

It roared like a freight train and it only took seconds to form a deep lake. Nothing floated to the top, not even them!

***

Nana, Judith, and David watched in a state of shock, not saying a thing! Before they could catch their breath they saw it! A white light shot through the water and up to the heavens. The light was so bright it lit up the grounds where the plantation once stood.

Steven came up first with Ty in his arms. She was limp when he took his first step out of the water onto the dry road. Kip was next, he had Sissy in his arms and she was choking and spitting out water. However, Dennis came up on his own. Steven laid Ty down and rolled her on her side to help drain the water from her lungs. Sissy, Kip and then Dennis stood over her with their eyes blazing. It was Sissy that stepped forward and bent down and touched her face.

"Breathe Ty…breathe!" Sissy said *mentally*.

Ty began to choke and fight for each breath.

"Nana said you were just like Mother Nettie, a healer, and that you are," Kip said to Sissy.

Ty was sitting up trying to get her bearings, but she was breathing.

"Thank you SI, Thank you!" Nana said.

***

Steven and Sissy were helping Ty to the truck and Dennis and Kip were walking behind them.

Kip stopped and looked directly at Dennis: "You just had to, didn't you?" Kip asked in anger.

"Don't act like you didn't want to, all of you did," Dennis said as he cut back at Kip with his words.

They stared at each other, then continued to walk to the truck. They all heard Uncle David say *mentally*: "Just go home. Drive careful Son and make it to Momma's house!"

***

CHAPTER 9 - A new day!

The sun was coming up as Steven opened the gates to the Montague Estate with very little *mental* effort. Everyone in the SUV was asleep, except Steven and Ty.

"Welcome home Steven," Ty said.

"And what a beautiful home it is. Ty this estate has so many resources and Dad and I have developed blueprints to utilize all of them."

"You know about the oil wells at the back of the property?" he asked.

"Yes, and the Natural Gas lines," Ty said.

"Well, Uncle DW drew up the contracts for Nana to sell the oil and you know my Dad did the blueprints for the oil lines. This place uses the Natural Gas to heat, cook and provide outside lighting. Last year Dad and I supervised the installation of the Solar panels for all the electrical power. Five years prior, Dad designed the Turbine Windmills that also power the estate. Ty, we took Nana completely off the grid." He said.

"So you're saying, no matter what's going on in this world; The Montague is self-sufficient?" Ty asked.

"Exactly, and in two weeks when everyone comes home for the harvest, we're installing the three satellite receivers, Wi-Fi, Satellite channels and no dropped cell calls," Steven said.

"I haven't touched my cell phone since we got here," Ty said with a giggle. Steven had to laugh too.

"Yeah, we have free unlimited minutes with the gifts we have." He said.

Ty and Steven smiled at each other and continued to laugh as Steven pulled the SUV to the back of the mansion and everyone began to wake up.

"Now that was one hell of a night!" Kip said.

"Crazy night but we got the job done," Sissy said.

"Sissy I was thinking, you're the Medical Specialist and you have the gift of healing, would you mind..." Steven asked.

"It would be my honor! Unfortunately, I can't put flesh where there is none."

"I'll reassemble their bones," Sissy said.

Just then they heard Nana, *mentally*.

"Sissy, I have put Mother's and the baby's burial clothes in the barn. Child, wire the bones together and have Ty help you." Nana said.

"Yes Ma'am," Sissy and Ty said.

They all heard Nana and Sissy and Ty took the backpacks into the barn and started the process. The men went into the back door of the mansion; into the kitchen where Judith and Nana were waiting.

Dennis entered first and fell down to his knees in front of Nana, placing his arms around her waist. As she held his head with both hands and looked into his gray eyes he said: "Nana, I tried to control my rage, but when that evil Bitch pointed that shotgun at Sissy..." Nana cut him off.

"We would be burying Sissy if you hadn't."

"We have the right to protect ourselves and to take what belongs to us. I just didn't know you alone could ..." Nana said as he cut her off.

"Nana, I noticed all the mud on the property and it hadn't rained in weeks. I knew that property was on a wetland sinkhole. It was going down anyway. I just helped it happen sooner." Dennis said.

Nana couldn't help but laugh, "you sure did."

"Boy get up and get out the way, trying to get all my Nana's love," Kip said in a playful manner.

Dennis got up and kissed Nana on her cheek as Kip pushed him out the way. Kip bent down and hugged Nana.

"Kip, Dennis did the right thing, so you need to let it go. Child I told you, you can't bargain with the devil. Sometimes you gotta fight fire with fire." Nana said.

"Uh huh Nana," Kip said, stealing Nana's sugar.

Steven was standing in the doorway with his gray eyes on a soft warm glow as he watched his cousins loving on Nana and Judith. Nana looked up and saw him and opened her arms.

Steven walked up to his grandmother, towering over her; all five foot one inch of Nana, overshadowed by all six foot five inches of cut, muscular, GQ, beautiful African Warrior, Steven! He lowered his head and slowly went down on one knee. As he spoke the word with so much bass it brushed her long thick gray tresses: "Nana!" Steven said as he looked up at her with his gray eyes glowing warm and affectionate.

"Steven, you are my first grandchild; looking the spitting image of your Father and him my Father."

"Forty years ago your Father put you in my arms and I knew you were special! No one could be the head of this new household, no one but you. Welcome home, Steven Kimtu Montague!" Nana said.

Steven took Nana's hands, kissed them and then placed them on his heart, "Thank you Nana!" he said.

"Your gift is exceptionally strong and Ty will compliment you well. You two are the Protectors, Overseers, and Warriors of the next generation. Together you will write new Chapters into The Learning. Ooh child, y'all got stories to tell. Fearless and Unstoppable you two are!"

"When you stepped out of that deep lake with Ty in your arms, I just knew...if you ain't my Father's..." Nana stopped.

She was trembling and shaking, but Steven held her tight as she laid kisses on his head.

"Nana, I feel him much stronger now that I'm here. I watched every moment of his retrieval and burial," Steven said.

"I know you did child, and you should feel stronger. The more of them we bring home the stronger you children will be. Your inheritance is being given to you." Nana said, but she had to change the subject because looking at Steven was like looking at his namesake, her Father.

"Now I know my men-children are hungry and tired, so go clean up children and come back and get your nourishment," Nana said.

"Yes Nana," They said in unison.

***

Sissy and Ty were in the barn. Sissy had placed all of Mother Nettie's bones in anatomical order on the table. Ty watched her carefully and shook her head in amazement.

"Damn Sissy, you're so good at this. It's only right your gift is of a healing nature." Ty said.

"Ty it feels like I was born for this. You know, like it's in my DNA." Sissy said.

"Not to change the subject, but ..." Ty said.

"What is it, Ty?" Sissy asked.

Ty had a big shit eating grin on her face.

"Remember when we were growing up and we would go stay at Uncle David's house for the summer. How we would wait till he went to work, then we would turn the stereo on and have his whole house rocking?" Ty asked.

"What the hell made you think of that?" Sissy asked.

"Do you think Uncle David knew?" Ty asked.

"Ty please, why do you think he whipped Kip's ass? Kip scratched up his "New Birth album." It's me for you, skip...skip, and you for me!"

"That was the first time I saw Uncle David smoke a joint." They both cackled hard as Sissy continued.

"Ooh I get it, you and Steven been talking and you're reminiscing. Ty have you noticed Steven, girl he...*with her gray eyes blazing* "I mean he my cousin...but...bae bae, Steven is ripped! Eyelashes looking like he wearing at least three coats of mascara, hair down his back, skin like dark Hershey chocolate, just FINE child FINE!" Sissy said.

Ty couldn't quit laughing. "Uh uh, you know you wrong for that Sissy, but you ain't never lied. Jesus, Steven is God given Fine!" Ty said.

They squealed with laughter and Sissy went back to work and Ty helped.

***

CHAPTER 10 - *In your dreams*

Sissy and Ty had finished assembling the bones of Mother Nettie and her son. Sissy placed Nettie into the burial cloth and sewed the arms out as the rest of her was sewn into a swaddling wrap. Her baby was completely sewn into a swaddling wrap, as well. Ty placed him into Mother Nettie's arms as they did the final wrapping to hold them securely into place.

Even though you couldn't see the faces; you

Ty Hamilton

could plainly make out the body figures of a Mother holding a newborn child.

In amazement, Ty and Sissy stepped back and held hands.

"Sissy this is absolutely beautiful," Ty said.

"It is so sad, but morbidly beautiful!" Sissy agreed.

"I know in my heart if every one of our Universal family could find their loved ones that suffered thru slavery…" Ty said as Sissy cut her off.

"They would do what we are doing; out of honor, love, and respect, because we stand on their shoulders," Sissy said.

"We owe them this. They deserve to be brought home, where they are loved and given a proper burial so they can rest in peace with their loved ones." Ty said.

Sissy and Ty stood there with tears in their eyes. They were thinking if they could have endured the indignity of slavery; then the barn doors opened on their own accord and the two walked out. They were tired and thankful. Together they peacefully walked into the kitchen for some well-deserved nourishment and rest.

***

Nana and Judith were outside on the porch rocking in their favorite chairs.

"Judith, like I told you, those children have strength and devotion on their side. They were absolutely right. I couldn't have made it on the Franklin Plantation. I probably would have died out there. Somehow they knew it was best for me not go." Nana said.

"Ooh and Steven…" Judith said.

"Judith I know. He looks just like a younger version of our Father. These new generation men of ours, they like to wear their hair long. Kip keeps his up in a ponytail like a Samurai and Dennis has some kind of twist looking braids all over his head. Steven wears his down his back when he doesn't have it up in that Saudi Arabian wrap." Nana said.

"But Nana, they are all muscular like men and there really isn't anything feminine about them," Judith said.

"Ooh no child, I'm not saying they don't look like men, they look like African Warriors. Well to tell you the truth, they are beautiful, each one with his own unique style." Nana said.

"Ooh yeah Nana, they fine!" Judith said.

"Where did you learn that from?" Nana asked.

"Sissy!" Judith said as the both of them

laughed.

"And speaking of Ms. Sissy; the Mother Nettie look alike and our new healer. That child, we got to get her married off and full up with babies," Nana said.

"Well Nana, you know your children are coming home for the harvest. Why don't we invite some of the families around here for a big party and introduce Sissy to some of these young men." Judith said.

"Judith you surprise me with your forward way of thinking. Fixing Sissy up and that ain't a bad idea after all." Nana said.

"Remember how your women friends fixed you up with your husband?" Judith asked.

"Ooh child, I remember everything about that man. He was my love, the Father of my children." Nana said, but quickly she went quiet because not all memories are good memories.

"It will be about time to tell them all about him in The Learning," Judith said.

"Real soon Judith, but first we gonna bury Mother Nettie at sunset. So let's let this be a peaceful day." Nana said.

No sooner than Nana said the words, Scotty and Rock came running by. They were playing like two bad children with a big wooden stick in their mouth. They pulled and tugged against each other for possession of it.

"Those two don't show up much, just for dinner. They act like they want to kiss my face when I'm bending down filling up their bowls with leftovers. I talk to them and when they are done eating, they come to me for petting." Judith said.

"Those two dogs know they are home and

they know their Montague's better than anyone else. The only thing missing with them is gray eyes." Nana said.

Nana and Judith had a good laugh as they continued their rocking and humming, while Scotty and Rock continued their rough housing. The birds were chirping and the flowers were open wide, alive and happy, that best explains what a beautiful day it is on the Montague estate.

***

Upstairs, Kip, Dennis, and Steven began to awaken. Sissy was sound asleep, but Ty's sleep was disturbingly interrupted. Her eyes were racing back and forth with movement. She was dreaming, but this was no ordinary dream. She's having a nightmare!

Steven stood up and stretched. He always started his day with push ups and sit ups, and today was no exception. Steven was thinking to himself that by agreeing to stay here in place of Nana, this would be for the rest of his life. He and Ty both knew they would forsake marriage and having children.

Ty had an ex-husband and he had an ex-wife. Both had married young. And on all accounts, they grew up and grew apart from their mates. Even though both of them had successful businesses, they both longed for family. To be the caretakers of the family and this estate; was the perfect solution for their needs.

Steven knew at sunset they would bury Mother Nettie, and he had slept longer than he intended. So it was to the shower, get dressed and spend time with the others.

He liked his shower cool and he loved to let the water flow down his long tresses; it soothed his mind but nothing could prepare him for Ty's disturbing link.

***

Ty's nightmare was so distressing, it shook her body. She was struggling. She was trying to push her body against intensely strong winds. The rain was so heavy, her clothes and hair were weighing her down. She could feel someone holding her hands and trying to get her to safety. It was Kip and Dennis.

To her right, she could see Steven holding Sissy's hand as he was desperately trying to pull her up to him. The storm was too strong! Ty had never seen anything like this.

Trees were uprooted and nearly hitting them, and then she felt Kip and Dennis losing their grip. Her fingers were slipping out of their hands as they moved forward and out of her sight.

Now she could see Sissy and Steven struggling to hold on to each other, but Sissy was behind him and slipped back behind them. She tried to link with them, but it wasn't working. Nothing was working!

The rain beat her face to the point she had to squint to see. And when she could see, she saw Steven reaching for her and the closer they got to reaching each other the stronger the rain and winds were.

Then she saw Steven being swept away in a water spout. She heard herself *mentally* scream his name: "**Steven, please don't leave me, Ste-ven!**" Ty screamed to him.

***

Steven had to steady himself with his hand against the shower wall. As soon as she *mentally* screamed his name he heard her and caught the link. The shower was beating down hard on his head. He felt himself struggling to reach her, but he couldn't grab her hand. Then he felt himself lifting up off the shower floor. He *mentally* screamed out her name:

"Ty, wake up...Ty!" and Ty violently woke up.

***

It was like the devil himself was chasing her. The top sheet went up in the air and Ty cleared it before it landed back on the bed. Steven immediately turned off the shower and threw on his shirt and pants as Ty jumped and swung around the room looking for and grabbing her robe. Steven reached for Ty's door handle just as she opened it, and her head ran into his chest.

He looked down at her as she looked up at

him. Both sets of gray eyes were blazing white. She couldn't even speak as he stepped into the room and she stepped back. He closed the door without touching it and sat her down on the edge of the bed.

Ty's hands were shaking uncontrollably as Steven kneeled down and held her.

"Ty, what the Hell was that?" he said with serious question in his voice and Ty's arms wrapped around his neck.

"A nightmare; I have never had one like that Steven. Did you see it?" She asked as she held on to him for dear life and spoke in his ear.

"As soon as you screamed my name, I caught the link," Steven said as he continued to hold her and whispered into her ear.

"Steven we had no power against it and we were losing each other."

"Your Father said to pay attention to the dreams that forecast danger. I couldn't even make out where we were. Only once did I dream like this, the night my mother and your mother died together, in that car accident." Ty said.

Steven's eyes went lifeless as he recalled that night. Two very important Montague women were taken with a turn of the screw. He had dreamed it too, the same time as Ty. Somehow, he and Ty knew they were destined to be together. Somehow, someway, it would always be them two.

Steven had to steady himself as he spoke: "Ty listen, I need you to pull yourself together. Since we are the only ones that have the gift of dreams, let's not panic the others until we figure this out." He said.

Ty wouldn't let go of Steven's embrace. Scared wasn't even the word, more like scared to death, to see people you love being ripped away from you and not being able to do anything about it. Just like the night she and Steven *mentally* stood there, holding hands and watched the life drain from their mother's bodies.

Steven saw all of Ty's thoughts as she remembered them. He could still feel the hurt and the helplessness they felt. He was ten years old and she seven. They were too young with their underdeveloped gifts and powerless to stop what was happening. Their scenario was like Nana's. That's how she knew these two Warriors would stay. Everything was falling into place, just like Nana knew it would.

That night, Nana had warned Andrew and David to stop their wives from going out. So instead of going to the French quarter, they decided to go to Baton Rouge for a night out.

They never made it across Lake Pontchartrain. They were rear-ended by a drunk driver and pushed up under the back of a tractor trailer. All the while, Ty, and Steven watched the whole horrible event.

Andrew couldn't remarry and David didn't either. They felt guilt. If only they had listened to their mother. Instead, they dismissed her warning, but never again. From that day forward, they never took any warning Nana gave them as a joke. It cost too much in the end!

Ty and Steven looked at each other with understanding. This family had its share of tragedy and loss, and they wanted no more. Steven looked at Ty as she finally spoke:

"This is something big and I don't think we can stop this."

"Steven, if a big storm comes, there's nothing we can do to stop SI's might," she said.

"But we don't know what it is and where it was. So we'll talk about this in private after the burial," he said.

"Ok, I hope I'm wrong," Ty said.

"I do too. Are you good now?" Steven asked.

"No, but I'll get it together." she said.

As Steven went to the door he looked back at Ty and smiled.

"You look like a beautiful black panther sitting there with your hair a mess," Steven said.

"Steven please, with your hair wet and dripping in your face, you look like a model in an Essence magazine." she said as both of them laughed to cut the tension.

As Ty sat there she could hear the others coming up to their rooms to prepare themselves for the burial. It was two hours before sunset and time to get ready.

***

CHAPTER 11 - Together again

Everyone was dressed in white and meeting up at the barn. Sissy had done wonders with the linen burial cloth and it truly was a sad but happy occasion. Sad, because of the way she was murdered with a child, as so many slaves had been murdered before her. They died in unthinkable, barbaric ways. The Southern and Northern soil is littered with their blood and bones. They were misplaced and lost to their families that loved them and longed to bring them to a resting place.

The new generation of Montagues would not let history repeat itself: SI first, family second.

All of them had sad but thankful faces. However, Nana looked weary of what was to come next. The next Learning would be of a love between a man and a woman. It would be her life story of great sorrow, perseverance, and triumph.

***

As the burial started, the formation was different this time. Dennis and Kip were at the right and left foot of Mother Nettie and Steven was at her head, as the head of the household should be. This time, the women followed behind.

It was a slow processional walk. And as they walked, all of them thought about how many slaves would never be properly buried.

***

The sun had set when they reached the crypt and the second white concrete casket was opening as Steven, Kip, and Dennis placed Mother Nettie and her baby boy inside.

Just then, Father Kimtu's Casket opened and a bright white light illuminated the entire crypt. Sissy was the first to go down, then Steven. It was as if they had been hit in the chest and knocked off their feet.

Dennis had Sissy's head on his lap but she was not unconscious and Ty held Steven's head on her lap, but he neither was unconscious. Their eyes were focused on the image of Kimtu holding his baby boy and Mother Nettie at his side. No one blinked at the sight of them!

"Steven, I have given you my gift and I appoint you the head of our family. You are truly my namesake. Very soon you will prove yourself to be a great warrior and worthy to lead the way for the next generations to come." Kimtu said.

"Sissy, I have given you my gift of healing. You are now the healer of our family! You have the heart and soul of a healer, and are most worthy to be appointed." Mother Nettie said.

"Nana and Judith my children, I love you beyond death and you have done well. Ana, let go of your guilt. You were a child and could have never helped me. It was my choice to fight. That I do not regret. I am free, never to be enslaved again."

"I thank you all for bringing myself, my wife and child together in our final resting place. We can finally rest in peace," Kimtu said as they stood there looking their normal selves.

Reunited for the last time. They were a complete family, in no pain, no more loss and no more tears.

Nana, Judith, and the children stood there and listened intensively to Father Kimtu's final words:

"There is nothing greater than love. So love each other, protect each other and be free my children. Free to believe in a God which nothing is impossible! Just believe in SI...and believe in yourselves."

With his final words, the lights dimmed and they saw both casket lids were closed. Steven and Sissy stood up with a little assistance, but Ty noticed

Steven had blood on his shirt.

"Steven you're bleeding. Sissy, help him!" Ty said.

Sissy opened his shirt and Steven looked down; everyone saw it and gasped. Steven had the same African tribal marking on his shoulder as Father Kimtu.

Sissy looked down at her chest and noticed the same mark on her. She took her hand and placed it over Steven's mark and the blood and soreness went away and Nana and Judith smiled.

"Children your gifts of inheritance have been given to you; you will need no more. Father and Mother are finally at rest, and Ty you will write this and every new story in The Learning." Nana said as Ty nodded her head in understanding.

"There is no more for us to do here, so let us

go home children," Nana said in conclusion.

They all left the crypt headed to the mansion.

"Unbelievable! Sissy and Steven are African Super Heroes." Dennis said jokingly.

"Hey Sissy, do you think you can cook up a Super meal because I'm starving." He said.

"Boy, I'm still your big sister," as she slapped him in the back of the head, "I will hurt you and then heal you," Sissy said jokingly.

Everyone was laughing at those two, as they *mentally* remembered Kimtu's final words:

"Love each other, protect each other and be free. Free to believe in a God which nothing is impossible! Just believe in SI...and believe in yourselves."

"Word!"

CHAPTER 12 - In Ty's Spot

After dinner everyone went to bed and slumbered peacefully, everyone except Ty. It had been three days since Mother Nettie's burial. And earlier that week, Ty's moving truck had arrived with all of her favorite furniture and office equipment. She had chosen to use the whole back half of the second floor of the mansion. It was like having a midsize house all to herself.

Steven had decided on the front half of the second floor, so they could always be close to each other, no matter what. After all, they were a team.

In Ty's suite, there is a white living room with a white fireplace and a white baby grand piano. So Ty's white sectional with pastel baby blue pillows, and platinum accessories completed it. As Dennis referred to it, it was her cloud room.

Also, she has a full kitchen with black marble countertops and black and white backsplash. If that wasn't enough; a master bedroom with a master en-suite bathroom, plus a room and a half of closet space. Yeah, this was Ty's spot and she loved it all, especially her Obama size office.

Ty loved to skype her calls because she was excellent at reading body language. Ms. Teresa (Ty) Montague was a sensitive thinker, a loner, and her surroundings were everything. That's just the way she is, a Wild Card, a free-thinking spirit. To tell the truth, she never cared much for controlling people. Their need for control was a dead giveaway to their insecurities. Never attempt to clip Ty's wings and all would be well.

When it comes to Steven, he has the analytical mind, a creative mind, able to envision his creations and mentally work out the details before making them tangible. Being the only child suited him well too.

Ty could be hard-headed and stubborn and so could he. Steven would listen to jazz when she would work on his nerves. And in return, she would give him the silent treatment when he pissed her off. He absolutely hated that shit! Steven always wanted to talk it out, but she would clam up on him and shut down shop. She really knew how to get on his last nerve. But at the end of the day, they were indivisible!

***

Working in her office was a welcome distraction from the dreams that came every single night. Thank goodness she had learned to handle the intensity of them. With each dream, she would uncover pieces to the big picture and she wasn't telling Steven or anyone about them. She just told them she had neglected her work and she had to put in extra time to catch up. It was more like all-nighters and not exactly about the work.

She was not sleeping at all because the dreams had become more horrifying. Ty was staying up all day and all night, living on coffee. It was a good thing she didn't like pills. Sometimes she would sleep in two-hour intervals, relying on her alarm to wake her before she could possibly start to dream. But sleep deprivation was right around the corner, and it would only be a matter of time before her body shut down.

***

Ty was sitting in her office looking at a pile of resumes for ads she had placed for help. She needed two pilots, able to fly a Gulfstream Jet and a Bell helicopter. And then there were the ads for a Chef and Housekeepers. She knew Nana and Judith were getting older. So it was her intent to remove as many chores as she could and make their lives as comfortable and relaxed as possible.

She had already skyped two applicants for pilots and she watched their body language very carefully. Both were licensed, reputable pilots. But what really got to her was they both were descendants of the Tuskegee Airmen.

Being as organized as Ty is, she had done pre-interviews and narrowed her search down. So tomorrow the family would be interviewing all day right here on the estate.

**

It had been hours since she had eaten anything and she sure would love to spend time with her favorite cousin, Ms. Sissy. Earlier, she had found her record collection and she had Rufus and Chaka Khan playing in the background. Ty knew Chaka was Sissy's favorite artist and she also knew as soon as Sissy heard it she would be on the way. Wait a minute 3...2...1 a knock at the door and Ty opened it and smiled. It was Sissy with a tray of food and a bottle of Nana's homemade peach wine.

"You rang!" Sissy said, sounding like Lurch on the Adams Family. She passed by Ty doing a Crip walk and singing a verse of "you remind me of a friend of mine."

Ty had to giggle, "That's my girl. You brought food and wine. Can I convince you to stay here with me and Steven?" she asked.

Sissy was still Crip walking. "I mean Steven's fine and all, but no child," she said in her Jamaican accent. "I gotta find me a Mon little one." as both of them started laughing and dancing to Chaka.

"Wow you allowed little old me up in the White House with your Tybama office; Madam President of the United Black States of America," Sissy said as they both cackled.

"Sissy you always make me laugh no matter what's going on," Ty said.

Sissy was still dancing and doing her Stevie Wonder head rolls.

"So Ty, what's ta matta, what's going on, Gurl?" Sissy asked in her full out Jamaican patois.

"Sissy you know Uncle David said I should pay attention to the dreams that forecast danger," Ty stated.

"Does that mean the Denzel dreams don't count," Sissy said as they both chuckled.

"I don't care what Pauletta say, she has him 24/7, hell I have to dream him up," Sissy said.

"Girl that man is beyond! Sorry love, you have to get your own. As for me, I want mine like Heavy D said: Black coffee, No sugar, No cream." Ty said as they fell back on the white sectional in laughter.

"Sissy seriously, I never told you about my dreams. I don't understand it yet, but they're nightmares. So do me a favor. Stay here with me and let me get some sleep. If you see me dreaming, please wake me up." Ty begged.

"Cool, until you're ready to talk about it. You sleep and I'll listen to some old school. If I see you dreaming, I'll wake you up." Sissy agreed.

As soon as Sissy hit the Isley Brothers – "Run for your guns," Ty was sleep!

***

CHAPTER 13 – Welcome

Ty woke up and it was the next day. "Sissy I love you with your healing ass," Ty said to herself.

That night Ty had no dreams and slept like a baby. "SI, bless Sissy for her goodness." It was a good thing, for today the family would be choosing the new staff members.

Ty took the best shower ever, put on her white sleeveless jumpsuit with a wide brown belt and her brown wooden necklace and white and brown wooden earrings. She had brushed her long black curls back off her face and tied a silk white scarf around her head.

Warm, bronze eyeshadow adorned her eyelids and black eyeliner gave her the smoky eyes that set those gray eyes ablaze. She applied burnt-orange lipstick to her seductive lips and slide her feet into her white and brown, three-inch spectator pumps.

As she left out of her room, she did her Naomi Campbell strut to the kitchen to join the family for breakfast. Dennis spied her first when she walked into the kitchen and did her Fashion Model, slow animated turn, threw her head back and did the Nae Nae Dance.

Dennis burst out in laughter:

"Lazarus has risen! And she looks fierce!"

he said.

Ty walked over to him and kissed and hugged him. Then she pulled his braided hair to snap his head back:

"Look here Dennis the Menace just because the men in this family are fine; doesn't mean the women look bad," Ty said.

Kip stood up for his kiss and hug.

"Ooh no, the women in this family are Beautiful. Especially that one over there," Kip said as he pointed to Nana, and Sissy and Judith stood up.

"Boy, you must be blind in those gray eyes. Ms. Judith and I are stacked!" Sissy said.

"Stacked!" Judith said as she extended her arm and snapped her finger.

Nana and everyone got the giggles as she saw her sister Judith being brought out of her shell with Sissy's badness. Nana knew Judith would be just fine without her.

Ty was half laughing when she said, "have you guys had time to go over the resumes? I hope so or we can go by our feelings." She said.

"I really like the two pilots," Steven said.

"Me too child," said Nana.

"Descendants of the Tuskegee Airmen; I bet them fly boys are bad!" Steven said.

"Ty I knew you had good taste, but do you know how special they are?" Nana asked.

"Yes Ma'am, and your baby girl got connections." as Nana and Steven smiled.

"They will be flying special cargo…my family. We have got to have the best fly boys' eva!"

Ty said as she and Steven pounded fist and exhale with a hiss.

"This Chef looks good on paper," Sissy said.

"Well Ms. Judith, wait till you meet him in person. I've asked him to cook for us." Ty said.

"Ooh fine and can cook too," Sissy said.

"Um, Sissy he's not for you, he's..." Ty said as she pointed at Ms. Judith.

Nana burst out laughing. She looked at Ty and laughed even harder.

"Get her Ty," Nana said as Ms. Judith blushed.

"Judith is always trying to fix someone up. Now she doesn't have anything to say." Nana added.

"Nana!" Judith said.

"Hush Child, ain't nothing wrong with you having a man friend for some company," Nana said.

"Exactly," Ty said as she agreed with Nana.

"Now, the housekeepers I leave to you, Nana. You know your house better than anyone, and there is no better judge of character than you. As a matter of fact, feel them all out. We have an hour before we take care of business and I'm hungry." Ty said.

The Montagues enjoyed their meals and conversations, but most of all, they enjoyed each other.

***

It was exactly one hour later and people started driving through the front gate. First, there was Captain Devin, aka Mr. D as he liked to be called. He was the son of a Tuskegee Airman that loved to fly. Captain Devin had raised his children and after his wife died he wanted to work in the private sector. Captain Devin would be the Jet pilot and the co-pilot for the Helicopter.

Behind him in a black Navigator was Cordell. He was the son of Captain Devin's only brother. Cordell was a Wildcard but had much love, respect, and admiration for his Uncle. Cordell would be the co-pilot of the Jet and the pilot of the Helicopter.

Chef London was behind Cordell. He had owned his own restaurant for thirty years and his sons and daughters ran it now. He could never retire from what he loved doing and Chef London was also a widower.

Finally, behind the Chef were Mrs. Carla and her four daughters. They wanted to work together and work for one family. Mrs. Carla was a widow trying to keep her family together.

As they exited their vehicles, everyone was welcomed by the family and their guests were pleasantly surprised to find the Montague's were a loving, respectful and wealthy African American family.

Ty and Steven took Captain Devin and Cordell to their office to discuss the Jet and Helicopter they had selected. They needed to finish the blueprints Steven had designed for the runway, helipad, and the airplane hangar.

Nana sat in the living room with Mrs. Carla and her girls going over the house and what was needed. Sissy and Ms. Judith took Chef London into the massive, modern kitchen to show him around. They were waiting for Dennis and Kip to join them so they could show Chef the livestock, fishery, orchards and vegetable gardens.

The delivery truck had pulled up and Dennis and Kip were surveying the four new, white canopy golf carts that Ty and Steven had purchased to make it easier for the staff to get around the estate.

**

After all the interviews, Nana called the children into the living room:

"Well, you wanted to know what I felt about the staff. Let's start with the two pilots. Captain Devin is a Father figure for Cordell. He only makes him better. Cordell loves to fly and respects his Uncle, but the day will come when Cordell will have to take the reins." Nana said.

"Captain Devin knows everything about aerodynamics. I believe he could land a plane safely on the edge of a mountain and Cordell would get the biggest thrill out of it. Cordell is truly a Wildcard, that's why he is perfect to pilot the Helicopter." Steven added.

"I think you're both right," Ty said.

"Ok, then there's Mrs. Carla. She's doing the

best she can for her daughters. They're growing up faster than she would like, but she can't stop SI's will for the living. Children, she needs our help and she's too proud to ask for it. So we need to make it a part of the arrangement. The woman has too much stress on her to provide a home and food for her family, and she's almost out of sacrifices." Nana said.

"Chef London, by the smell of things, that man knows his way around some collards and poke salad," Nana said.

"Nana if he doesn't feed us soon..." Ty said.

"Yeah Ty I know, he just has to accept our offer," Steven said as he smiled at Ty.

"That man loves to please thru his cooking, but it's something else. He's lonely and Judith reminds him of his wife. He will love being in a full house and spending time with her." Nana concluded.

"So that settles it. We make our offer and include the houses on the property." Steven said.

"But not before I tell them about our family and our gift. That's something we don't hide on our land. If anyone wants to leave, then now would be the time." Nana said as Steven and Ty agreed.

"Steven gather everyone into the kitchen and I'll tell them what they need to know," Nana said.

Chef London had laid out a spread and everyone ate, really ate. His pleasure was written all over his face. Everyone thanked him for a delicious meal and Nana started telling them about the family. She saved our gift for last. To our surprise, everyone there had ancestral stories. They had heard many stories about magic and voodoo. But they were God fearing people, and so is The Montagues. By any name, God is God, and there is only one true God.

Nana explained Ty and Steven's union. She made it clear that Steven was the head of the household and in his absence, or to his assistance, next in command was Ty. Nana even stated that she didn't know how much longer she would last, but she wanted to be surrounded by love and the company of good God fearing people.

Ty and Steven handed each person their offer and Mrs. Clara was the first to accept. Sissy and Dennis took her and her girls outside to pick the house of their choice. Next, Chef London accepted and Judith and Kip took him off to show him his new home.

Finally, Captain Devin asked specifics about their gifts. Nana smiled at him and looked at Ty and Steven and then their eyes lit up. Captain Devin pushed away from the table and Cordell stood up in a defensive manner.

"Son, you really want to sit back down. You couldn't imagine what my children are capable of doing." Nana said.

Cordell sat down cautiously, never taking his eyes off Ty. She smiled and winked at him as her and Steven's eyes went to their normal state. It was then that Nana *mentally* said:

"I can show you better than I can tell you."

She shot a *mental* vision to Captain Devin and Cordell. She showed them how her Father was murdered, then how they had brought him home and his burial. Next were Mother Nettie's murder, rescue, and burial.

Then she spoke out loud: "We use our gift to defend ourselves, to take what is ours and for the good of the people that live on this land with this family."

Captain Devin visually had to steady himself because of the injustice he just witnessed and the beauty of this family's unity to bring their family members home for a burial that was so rightfully deserved, and that so many would not receive.

"If you didn't have this gift you would have perished like so many others," he said.

"Captain Devin, I was born a slave and I've seen more evil vile things done to our people than these gray eyes ever want to see again. But let me assure you, I will die a free woman surrounded by my loved ones."

"My love for all my children is more important than my own life because they are our future," Nana explained.

"So will you stay and keep my loved ones safe in those flying machines?" Nana asked.

"It will be my honor." he said.

Then Cordell spoke in full understanding, "me too."

Ty and Steven were standing at the door waiting to show them their new homes as Nana sat there sipping her coffee, humming and tapping her cane.

***

CHAPTER 14 - Kip, you're gonna get it

Last night Ty didn't sleep at all. She resorted to working the night away. With the addition of the new staff members, there were college scholarships to set up for Mrs. Clara's four daughters. She also was having the Jet customized. She and Steven had decided the Jet would be customized with the "M" marque sewn on all the seats.

Chef would need a freezer and two electric burners in the galley. Steven wanted the Jet painted white with blue pin stripes on the sides, and MTQ1 painted in blue on the tail for the call letters. As for the helicopter, Steven referred to it as the MTQ2 and Ty took care of all the details.

Ty had skyped Aunt Pam in Chattanooga; she handles all their financial needs. Some people are great with money matters and Pam was one of them. Nana had sent her daughter to college specifically for Estate Accounting. In addition to the estate, Pam would also handle Ty and Steven's business accounts. Nana knew Pam was a worthwhile investment.

Nana had invested well in all her children and they were her greatest assets. DW was also a major player. He is an Attorney at law with his own law firm.

He personally handles all the legalities of the estate, and now Steven and Ty were placing their businesses under his care.

Andrew, Ty's father is a Building Contractor with his own company. He has the knowledge and the resources to build anything that David and Steven could put on blueprints.

David, Steven's father is an Architect in New Orleans.

Ruthie is a Performing Arts Professor, and her husband John is the principal of a Senior High School in Harlem, where they live. They are also Kip, Dennis and Shari's parents.

Kip is a successful Stock Broker in Manhattan, and Dennis is a Professor of African American Studies in Harlem, where he lives with his parents.

Of course, Ms. Sissy is a Registered Nurse,

specializing in Trauma Care. Sissy resides in Ohio, not far from DW and his brother Andrew.

Ty had spent fifteen years in Radio and Television and started her own successful production company.

Tomorrow all of Nana's children and their spouses would be here. Each and every one of them came home to spend time with their Mother and tend to the estate.

***

The staff was up and about working. They had the procedure down to a science. From Nana's personal experience during slavery days, she knew exactly how to successfully run a household.

It was now 8:00 am and Ty was exhausted. She hadn't slept at all for fear of her nightmares. Ty's stomach told her it was time to eat, so off she went, downstairs. She ran into Steven headed in the same direction, towards the kitchen.

"I smell Chef London is at it again. I don't know Ty, we're gonna have to start taking a morning run after breakfast each day." Steven said.

"That's a great idea. Starting today us children, *smiling at Steven*, should all do that. We really need to eat right and stay in shape. I have a feeling this next rescue and recovery will be hard on us all." Ty added.

"Speaking of eating right and staying in shape; there's also the matter of getting a good night sleep. Listen Ty, I'm not stupid. Even though you haven't spoken to me about your dreams; I link to you when you have them. I have been helping you manage them because they are so extreme, but for days at a time, you haven't been sleeping." Steven said.

Ty was avoiding Steven's ever knowing glare.

"I didn't know you were linked into my dreams. As far as not sleeping, I had to handle the details of the business. You know I do my best work at night. Steven, I didn't know you were adjoined to me." Ty said in surprise.

"Ever since Kimtu gave me his gift, my senses have been heightening to you. After all, we have been delegated as the Overseers of the family, and all things concerning. You and I feed off of each other and until you receive your final gift, yes you have yet to receive it, then you will be linked to me, the same way I am linked to you." Steven said.

"So you also know what I know about this next rescue and recovery?" Ty asked.

"Yes, I know. I wish I didn't. It's inevitable, and we will all face the inevitable one day."

"As for now, I need you to take better care of yourself. We will have to stay in shape, and that starts today. I need for you to sleep. If not, your body will shut down and rest on its own, at the wrong time." He said.

"Goodness Steven, you sound like a parent or a husband," Ty said.

"I'm both. You're my soulmate and if you go down, I go down. Do you understand what I'm saying? Kimtu was doomed because no one could help him. Nana tried but her gift was young and undeveloped. He knew this, but he made sure I wouldn't have the same fate. He knew that you would be the one to protect and nurture me if I fall and vice versa. Get it?" he asked.

"Not completely, but I'm starting to Learn." she said.

"Well, you will. So after breakfast, we're going for a run. This becomes a part of our daily regimen to be physically ready. Every day it is important for us to communicate everything to each other. We'll do this in private, away from everyone else, everything Ty! Your dreams are real and we have to decide just exactly what we can do with this knowledge. We can't save the world, but we can't sit by and do nothing." Steven said.

"I totally agree. Even though I have been getting bits and pieces, it's becoming very clear as to what it is and when and where it will happen." Ty said.

"Don't be afraid to sleep, your dreams don't last all night. Just know I am right there with you, and you have only to call me, and I will protect you," he said.

Ty was smiling at Steven when she replied, "well I won't be going to bed at 10:00 pm like you. You know I'm a night owl." She said.

Steven had to laugh.

"In Africa, you would have been the night lookout while your Warriors slept and replenished themselves. That's what you do for me. I don't need eight hours of sleep, but you're up holding down this warrior and when you sleep, I hold it down for you." he said.

"This warrior is starving! So can we please get breakfast and take that run. Oh, and today, can we go out to the runway site? I would like to see how this all works?" Ty asked.

"Of course we can. I have an emergency plan that you need to know about. So let's go eat and then we'll go for a run." he said.

***

As Ty and Steven entered the kitchen everyone was sitting at the counter while Chef London made fresh, homemade pancakes with slices of smoked ham. He had picked fresh strawberries and blueberries and adorned their plates with them. Nana was sitting there smiling as she saw them, and continued sipping her coffee.

"Well did everyone get their fill?" Chef asked as they all nodded yes in between bites.

"Do I have any special request for dinner?" Chef asked.

"Chef, I sure would like some fresh fish and I'm partial to lemon cake if you don't mind," Nana said.

"Nana I'm gonna work you up a feast. I'll get some crawfish too.

That is if Ms. Judith doesn't mind going with me to the fishery?" Chef London asked.

"Ms. Judith will join you and so will I," Dennis said, as he looked at Nana and smiled.

Dennis is smart to the ways of men, and he had made up his mind that no one disrespects Nana or Judith. As far as that goes, no one will ever force or take advantage of any of the women in his family. And Chef will soon find out that Dennis has made this his purpose.

"I think that would be a good idea. Judith, you need to get some fresh air, and Dennis, you can help the Chef catch them fish and crawdads."

"Why don't y'all take a picnic lunch and enjoy yourselves," Nana said.

"I want to go too," Sissy said.

"Then it's settled children, y'all go and have a good time. Mrs. Clara will keep me company, and Kip, Ty, and Steven; y'all got things to do. Cause children, tomorrow all Nana's babies are coming home. We got to get this place ready." Nana said.

***

After finishing breakfast, Kip, Ty, and Steven agreed to meet out back for their workout.

"Ok you two, why are we working out. What's going on?" Kip asked.

"You're ex-military, so you know the importance of staying in shape. And with Chef cooking like this; we need it more than ever," Steven said.

"Ok I'm down for a run, but after that, I've got to call my Lady. She's probably going nuts. Ty, you know how women get." Kip said.

"No I don't know Kip," she replied, sarcastic as hell. "Seeing that you; Samurai Warrior, change women like you change your suits, Mr. Wall Street! What I see is insecurity. She knows she won't last long, any longer than the others. Man when you gonna stop this?" Ty asked as she cut him with her words.

Steven turned his back to the both of them as Kip and Ty stared at each other. Kip was is in a state of shock as to how she knew his business and was cutting into him with her gray eyes. Kip was starting to get the realization that it's not the women, it's him.

Mentally they heard Nana-speak.

"Just shut your mouth Kip. Don't say another word. You know she's right. You don't argue with a panther when they're annoyed with you. Ha-ha, Ty you are becoming like me, little Nana." She said.

"Well, as usual, Nana has spoken her piece," Steve said.

And off they went. Steven and Kip were in front and Ty brought up the rear. Ty is a lot like Nana. When she speaks her mind she doesn't apologize for it. The truth is the truth, and it cuts deep.

Kip is in his late thirties and has had more than a man's share of women. It's time for him to stop playing games and feeding his ego, based on his looks. How shallow is that? Ty knows it's his fear of commitment but he needs a wake-up call.

"Damn man, am I that bad?" Kip asked as he was trying to find some empathy from Steven.

"Yes and more! You're wasting your years. Years you can't get back, being a playboy. Do you think after all Kimtu went through he would approve? Is that your purpose in life?"

"A lover of yourself, not caring about the feelings of others, is that you?"

"You treat women like they are items for your pleasure. How would you feel if a man treated your sister like that? Using her body for his pleasure, not caring about her feelings and then discarding her like yesterday's newspaper." Steven asked.

"Do you think you're more man than Dennis and me? If we wanted to be playboys we could do it too. But brother let me tell you, my penis does not control my life and never will. Besides, you know mine is bigger than yours" Steven said with a shitty grin.

"Ty's got you on point. **You're one hundred percent self-centered and selfish!**" he yelled.

Kip stopped and Steven and Ty keep running.

Ty moved up to Steven's side, and neither one of them looked back.

Once again, Nana *mentally* laughed and spoke her mind. "Kip git your ass back here and you come directly to me! You hear?" Nana asked.

"Yes Ma'am," He said.

***

Ty and Steven were standing at the spot for the landing strip.

"Look Ty, all of this will be a landing strip. It's four miles long with taxi strips to the mansion and the hangar. But what our pilots don't know is we can assist them with taking off and landing from any-where they are." Steven said.

Ty couldn't help but smile at Steven. "So our cargo is always safe?" She asked.

"Yep! My Dad and Uncle Andrew will start the work when they get here," Steven said.

"Also we need to do something about the river across the street," Ty said.

Steven put his arm around her shoulders. "I have told my Dad about that and he finished the lay-out. We will do as much as we can Ty, but a building does not make us a family, just remember that." Steven said.

"Steven have I told you how much I love you, with all my heart. Kimtu couldn't have picked a better man to be the head of the household. Like Sissy said, it's like it's in your DNA. Everything you have been through has prepared you for this time." she said.

Steven felt himself getting embarrassed by Ty's blunt praises.

"Thank you little one. You're also a perfect

fit. You're my right hand. You let me lead and if you disagree, then you speak your mind and I listen. You show me great respect and I appreciate that. It lifts me up. Oh, and I love you too, with all my heart." Steven said.

They smiled and walked towards the house as Steven had his arm wrapped around Ty's shoulders, and Ty was hugging him around his waist. They are the perfect pair of Warriors, and they are starting to understand the purpose of their lives.

***

Kip returned to the mansion and entered the back door. Nana was sitting in the kitchen, tapping her cane and waiting for him. Kip started to speak, but Nana motioned with her thick African cane for him to sit down, right there.

This moment reminded him when she would

administer discipline if he had been misbehaving. Little and loving as she was, she could put the fear of SI in your ass, and Kip knew this was one of those times.

"Kip I want you to listen, and listen well. Your cousins love you and want you to be happy, so do I. I'm going to talk to you so you can understand. **Boy, you need to stop this foolishness**! You're longing for love. Don't you know unconditional love is right here for you; where it has always been?"

"You make me sick with this material, success nonsense. You think if you live here and have this and do that, it makes you better than your family and others. You have lost sight of where you come from, and the hell it took to get here."

"Money and material things don't care for you. We do! If you lose everything, you can always come home, unconditionally without judgment. You have always thought that Dennis and Sissy were to follow you. And when they didn't, you thought that they were lower than you. The truth is, they know more than you do. They never ever stopped loving you and they never ever judged you for your mistakes. Oh yes, you have made mistakes, but you didn't learn a damn thing from them." Nana said blatantly.

Kip's head was lowered and he couldn't even look into Nana's blazing eyes.

"I'm gonna tell you this one time, and one time only: I'm not gonna be here for long. Don't cry out of guilt when I'm gone. Cry because you'll miss me. **Learn to forgive and change your ways boy, before you find yourself all alone!**" She yelled.

"Now go call this woman and speak like a

man. If you want her, tell her. If you don't, then set her free to find a love that she deserves." Nana said.

It took all of Kip's energy to stand up as Nana spoke again. "Now come over here and give Nana the love I know you can give." She said.

Kip fell to his knees in front of Nana, and Nana wrapped her arms around him and kissed him all over his face. She told him how much she loved him. It was then that Kip realized he had his own Learning to get, and he was receiving it.

Through his tears, he heard every word Nana said. And he didn't move; they stayed like that for a while, with Nana hugging him and humming her song. It was just like she did when he was a little boy.

***

CHAPTER 15 - No rest!

Dennis was parking the golf cart, and Judith and Sissy were giggling like two school girls when they got out. They started removing the bounty of food just as Ty and Steven walked into view.

"Where you two been? You should have been with us. Dennis so nuff can fish, and Chef caught enough crawfish to feed all of Louisiana." Sissy said.

"Chef you got us out here running this good food off," Steven said.

"It's been a long time since I saw my cooking make so many people happy, especially Nana. She always finishes her meal with a cup of my coffee, pats her cane and hums her song." Chef said.

"If you make Nana happy, you make us happy," Ty said.

"Fo sho! That's the secret to this family, Nana." Dennis said and they all agreed.

"Sissy I need to speak to you. Come and walk with me for a minute." Ty said.

As Sissy and Ty walked towards the orchard, the rest of the family entered the back of the house into the kitchen, to be greeted by Nana.

"Nana where is Kip?" Dennis asked.

"Ooh child, he had to make some phone calls

and we had a talk," Nana said.

Now everyone knew what that meant, except Chef. A talk with Nana meant you got your ass chewed.

So without saying anything, they went on about their business showing Nana the fish Dennis caught, and the fresh vegetable and the crawfish. Nana was smiling as she listened to Dennis's stories about how big the fish are, and how he caught all of them.

***

"Ok Ty, what's going on?" Sissy asked.

"I need a favor. Will you stay with me tonight so I can get some sleep?" Ty asked.

"Damn Sis, the dreams again?" Sissy asked.

"To be honest, I'm scared to dream."

"I just want to have one more night of good sleep before the rest of the family comes in tomorrow," Ty said.

"Ty damn, you know Steven's got your back. Hell, Stevie Wonder could see that when you two walked up looking like the dynamic duo." Sissy said.

"Sissy, please!" Ty begged.

Sissy paused and thought about how Ty needed to get over this fear shit. She couldn't possibly be afraid of a funky dream and if she is; what kind of Warrior is she gonna be.

"Nope! Nope! Nope!" Sissy said with conviction.

Ty was standing there like she had just been slapped.

"Ty you need to Warrior up."

"If you're afraid of this dream then you need to tell Nana, and get right! What kind of Warrior is afraid to sleep?" Sissy asked.

Ty quickly became pissed off at Sissy.

"You have no idea what I have not told you, or shown you, so your ass can sleep without worry. That's what kind of Warrior I am. **I have not said a word because I am protecting you and everyone else from what is about to come**!" Ty yelled.

"Ty I..." Sissy tried to speak as Ty cut her off.

"I'm sorry; if I'm not talking about a man you ain't interested...**I'm so sssick of her old black African Ass**." Ty said as she stormed off talking to herself, and left Sissy standing there with that "what the hell" look all over her face.

"Oh, I know her ass is tired. Go off on me like that, and walk away."

"Then dream on heifer, dream on! I hope you have the worst nightmare ever!" Sissy yelled at Ty because she was pissed off too.

As Ty entered the kitchen everyone felt the tension. She told Chef that she will take her dinner in her room. She said it was because she had work to do before the family arrived tomorrow.

Nana said she would have one of Mrs. Clara's girls bring it up. But nothing gets passed Nana and Steven these days.

So when Sissy entered the house minutes later, they notice she was trying hard to hide her emotions.

Steven *mentally* told Nana: "Those two just had an argument. About what was the question?" he asked.

All day it seems that Ty had been short with

everyone and Nana noticed it all. Something about her dreams, well if she wouldn't talk to Nana, then Nana would take a peek when Ty went to sleep.

***

As the family finished dinner, Chef started making Ty's plate and Sissy was making her a pot of coffee. Sissy had been collecting herbs and making medicine like Mother Nettie did, and Ty was having trouble sleeping. Since Sissy and Ty were like sisters, Sissy decided she would give her a little something to make her sleep and get back to normal.

***

Mrs. Clara's daughter took the tray of food and coffee up to Ty's room. Ty thanked her, smiled and closed the door.

Ty lit into the dinner and started drinking the coffee, one cup at a time.

It was going on 4:30 am and Ty was entering new stories into The Learning Book. She decided to take a shower, get into the sauna and drink some more coffee to make it till morning when the family made it in. It was 5:45 am and Ty's gray eyes would not focus. She fought it off and kept on working until her head hit the desk.

As her vision got blurry, she stumbled into her bedroom and remembered what Steven had said, "rest and you have only to call my name and I will protect you." So begrudgingly she went to sleep.

It was 7:00 am and everyone was stirring about. Chef was in the kitchen prepping for breakfast. Dennis and Kip were up taking showers. Steven was up doing his pushups, and Sissy was brushing her hair.

Mrs. Clara and her daughters were preparing

the third-floor bedrooms for the expected guest, but Nana and Ty were sound asleep. Ty had been asleep for less than two hours now. Two hours was the time she would start having the horrible dreams, but this time, she was not alone.

***

The front gate was being opened by Nana's children and everyone knew what that meant. Uncle David was ahead of the pack.

He had a truck full of Steven's belongings following him as he drove Steven's car, a Rolls Royce Dawn. Uncle DW and his wife Barbara, aka Bootsy, were next. Uncle Andrew was behind DW with his crew of workers, a concrete truck, and two big rigs hauling asphalt, a steam roller, and a backhoe.

The rest of the family was flying out at noon and would be there in time for dinner.

The children were standing on the steps to the mansion watching the arrival of their loved ones. As Uncle David parked Steven's Rolls Royce; he was greeted by Sissy, Kip, Dennis and his Son.

Uncle DW parked behind the truck and helped his wife out of the car. Uncle Andrew was right behind them, and they all walked into the loving arms of their family.

"Steven, where is Mama and Ty?" Uncle David asked suspiciously.

***

CHAPTER 16 - I can't let go

Ty had been asleep for exactly two hours and she was starting to dream. She was watching Nana on the plantation. Ty was seeing Nana as a young woman, and she was headed to the sugar cane fields. How could Nana be young and why was she here? Nana was singing a song, the same song she's always humming. No one knew, but the song was a love song from her husband Dan.

Dan knew his wife's code and he knew just how to answer her and let her know he was on his way. But something was wrong with the sky.

The sky was quickly changing from a beautiful clear blue to approaching darkness moving swiftly over the sugar cane fields.

Ty was calling Nana's name, but Nana didn't hear her. She called for Grandfather Dan, but both of them didn't notice her. Ty ran thru the fields in search of Nana, knowing she couldn't have gotten too far. As she ran towards Nana's singing; the field got darker and her eyes brighten, but the winds had picked up and she was struggling against the sugar cane.

In her sleep, she was struggling to run faster, as a powerful storm was coming, and now she could hear the sound of the mighty Mississippi on the other side of the field. It was swelling, and she was racing to beat the waves that she could feel was headed towards Nana and Dan.

The wind was pushing her from side to side, and her bed was smacking her bedroom walls from left to right, imitating the strength of the wind. Inside her suite the sectional was moving in the same rhythm as her bed, crashing from wall to wall. The wind gust became so strong that the long tall sugar cane began whipping her arms, her legs, her face, it was entangling her.

The more she struggled the more violent the whipping became. She could hear herself scream in pain!

Nana and Dan were holding each other and didn't seem to notice the storm and the rain, or Ty. The sugar cane had bound her arms and her legs and was whipping at her back. It sliced thru her clothes and cut her. She screamed out in excruciating pain! Then her gray eyes blazed a red hot flame and set the field on fire, which freed her.

She got up and started running towards them. She was getting closer as she felt the blood streaming down her face, her back, down her legs and arms. Her body felt heavy as she got within arm's reach of Nana. Nana's eye turned away from Dan and looked directly at Ty as she grabbed her and the wave of water hit all three of them.

The wind in Ty's room was so heavy it held her down on the bed, as everything inside flew around the room. But Ty did not wake. She held strong to Nana, and Nana held strong to Dan.

The wave held them under until it started pulling back towards the river.

Ty was reaching for a tree to stop them from being sucked across the street and into the mighty Mississippi. As she was reaching, she realized she couldn't hold on to it without letting go of Nana, and that she would never do.

In her mind, she remembered the graveyard would be coming up before they would be drawn back into the sugar cane field and across the street. She was pulled chest first into a concrete crypt and it knocked the air out of her. But it stopped her motion, and she held on to Nana for dear life.

Nana turned and looked at Dan in sheer desperation. She was losing her grip on him and he wasn't trying to hold on.

"Ana you have to let go of me. Let me go and go with Ty." Dan said.

"Ty doesn't need me, but you and I belong

together. If I die, I want to die with you," Ana said.

"You will not die with me, I'm already dead. Wake up my love. Wake up Ana." he said.

Nana turned to look at Ty. "Let me go Ty. Let me die with Dan." She begged.

But Ty would not let her go, and she screamed at Ty with total defiance.

"LET ME GO!" Nana screamed.

The water had pulled back to the river, but Ty didn't loosen her grip on Nana. She would not let her go because Ty knew this was just the beginning of the storm. The river was swelling for an even bigger wave as Nana turned to look at Dan. She and Ty saw him at the same time. Dan was decomposing in front of them.

"Ana you can't hold on to me because if you do, you will surely die."

"Go with Ty, the children need you," Dan said.

"But I need you," Ana said.

"It's too late, too late for me," Dan said as he decomposed into a pile of bones.

Nana looked at Ty and screamed from the agony in her heart, and Ty screamed back at her.

"Wake up Nana! Steven, help me! Don't let Nana die!" Ty yelled *mentally*.

***

As soon as she screamed his name, the front second-floor windows busted outward, and Steven caught her link.

But it was too late, the second wave was above their heads as Ty looked up she braced herself against the crypt, but Nana was twisting away from her.

The glass from the broken windows startled everyone outside, except for Steven. He had a shield over him as glass fell to the steps like rain.

Steven was taking the steps three at a time, and Kip, Dennis, and Sissy were right behind him, as he headed towards Nana's room. He yelled for Dennis to go upstairs and wake Ty.

***

They could hear the wind blowing inside Nana's room and the movement of furniture. Steven went to open the door but it wouldn't budge. Kip and Sissy linked with him and could not dislodge it. Steven felt himself fill with Kimtu's power and as he went to raise his hands, the tips of his hair turned gray from the brightness of his eyes and the door shattered into wooden shards. As they entered the room, Nana lay asleep in her bed and Sissy rushed to her side.

Steven called to her *mentally*.

"**Wake up Nana, get out of Ty's dream!**" he yelled, and Nana woke up!

Her heart was racing and she was fighting for air, but Sissy placed her hand on Nana's chest to slow her heart rate and Nana started breathing normally. She looked scared as she spoke to them *mentally*. "Where is Ty?" Nana said.

Steven broke for the door and up the stairs, as Nana's children rushed to Nana's room. Dennis was pushing on the door but he didn't have the *mental* or the physical strength to get into her room.

Steven pushed him out of the way as his eyes blazed to a hyper-glow and Ty's door swung open. Steven pushed into the wind and walked forward as the door slammed shut behind him!

Ty was still dreaming, but this time, the location had changed. Steven stumped through the heavy winds in sheer determination, as he *mentally* pushed furniture away from his path. He reached the doorway of Ty's bedroom to look upon her covered in blood.

She had open cuts on her legs and arms; and a deep cut was on the side of her face, as she was thrashing about on her moving bed. Steven *mentally* stopped the bed and wrapped Ty into the sheets.

With her in his arms, he backed up to the wall and lowered himself in the corner of the room, all the way to the floor. There he sat with Ty in his arms rocking her to comfort the violent thrashing.

As Steven closed his eyes and held her tight, he *mentally* called out to her.

"Ok Ty, it's you and me. Let's face this demon that is haunting you." He said and they linked.

CHAPTER 17 – Three months

Ty and Steven were holding hands and standing on a vacant Interstate 10. It was early Monday, August the 29th and Ty squeezed his hand, just like she did the night their mothers passed away.

"Steven, now I know what my dreams mean. It's two of them and they're less than one month apart." Ty said.

"Don't be afraid Ty, just show me," Steven said.

Ty led him thru a maze of abandoned vehicles on the highway. She started to climb a tractor trailer, and he followed her. They climbed on top of it so he could have a clear view. The sky had darkened again, but this time, the wind was pushing up from the Gulf, and with it came a surge of water, blinding rains and every creature that resided in it.

There were people still here. They didn't have the means to heed the warnings. Some had nowhere to go. The sky was completely dark now and Ty and Steven used their eyes to light up the night. She had to show him the destruction of homes, and of human life. As Steven watched, he gasped as the levees broke and swallowed up section after section.

There were people on their roofs taking the

brunt of the storm without shelter. There were people inside of their homes, too young, too old and too scared to leave. Ty buried her face into his back; she didn't need to see it again, she had been seeing it every single time she dreamed.

The days passed and still no help for the people. The heat and humidity were suffocating and the stench of cadavers made Steven heave.

No electricity, no fresh water. It had only taken days for society to break down. Survival was primal and it was each man for himself. The elderly didn't have a chance. They were dying from the heat, starvation and a lack of life-giving medicine, or medical care. The children were perishing as families were struggling just to stay alive. Bodies were floating in five to six feet of sewer water filled with rats, alligators, and snakes, but still no help.

People with Godly principles were trying to help others, but it was just too many and for days on end, no help! Places thought safe were overcrowded. Families, children, the elderly were at the mercy of criminals, murders, rapist, pedophiles, thieves, and no one came to help!

It was like the slaves on the plantation, existing in deplorable conditions. Being whipped, raped, and killed. No one cared and no one came to help!

Days had passed and it happened again! Steven's gray eyes filled with tears as he spoke the words.

"No help!"

Now he knew Ty's dreams and why they were so horrific. He turned to Ty and their tear filled eyes met up.

"They will call them, Katrina and Rita."

"Steven, this is what will cause the water to overtake Nana and her land, the lack of a levee," Ty said.

"We have family in this city and there are descendants of Africans here, our Universal family. We can't save them all, but we will not sit and watch. We will help them!" Steven said with conviction.

"We have only three months and that's all!" Ty said.

As soon as they finished speaking, Ty woke up. She looked up in Steven's face, wiped his tears and laid back down in his embrace!

"Steven, there's one more thing you're not seeing, Baton Rouge. Baton Rouge in years, they too will see flooding and we will need to help them as well." Ty stated.

***

Chapter 18 - Right as Rain

Ty and Steven stayed together like that, on the floor with their eyes closed, listening to each other breath. After all they had seen; they both knew it was inevitable! Downstairs in Nana's room, she was surrounded by her Sons, Kip, Dennis, and Sissy.

"Nana you're alright now," Sissy said.

"Yes child, but I need for you to get my healing balm."

"Go upstairs and work on Ty. Oh and Sissy…" Nana said.

"Yes Ma'am," Sissy said as she waited for Nana to speak.

"No more putting your Ju Ju herbs in Ty's or Steven's coffee," Nana said.

Sissy looked shocked, but then her face returned to normal. Why should she be shocked, Nana knew everything?

"Children, y'all help Nana get up from here and let's all get some of Chef's breakfast," Nana said.

Mrs. Carla and her girls were behind them cleaning Nana's room. They didn't ask any questions and they were not about to. They had a home and her daughters had a future. She was alright with not knowing because the Montagues had been good to them.

Judith had stayed in the kitchen with Chef, numbing him to what was going on in the house. She praised his cooking and kept him focused on getting things ready for the family.

"Chef everyone is on their way for breakfast, but I think we better make two trays for Ty and Steven. They will be joining everyone, later on, today." Judith said.

"Ok Judith, you know what's best," Chef replied as he smiled at her.

Sissy went up the steps to Ty's suite and before she could knock, Steven *mentally* opened the door for her. As she walked in, she saw how destructive Ty's dreams really were. As she got to the bedroom she could see Steven's black jeans and Timberland boots. But when she came thru the doorway she saw Ty wrapped in bloody sheets.

Immediately she kneeled down to check on the both of them.

"Ty I'm gonna take good care of you. I have Nana's healing balm and I didn't mean to..." Sissy said as Ty cut her off.

"Wish this on me," Ty said.

"And put your sleeping herbs in her coffee," Steven added.

Sissy looked shocked at her transparency, "I'm sorry; I never meant to hurt her." She said.

"That's why we have to be responsible with our gift." Steven scolded her.

"I forgive you, do you forgive me?" Ty asked.

"I love me some you," Sissy said with a smile.

"Back at you, but Sissy I'm so sore. Would you..." Ty said as Sissy placed her hand on Ty's forehead and she went silent.

Her eyes were unfocused as if she had been given a good shot of morphine.

"Ok Steven, bring her into the bathroom and I'll make her right as rain," Sissy said.

Steven rose up with Ty in his arms and followed Sissy.

***

Chapter 19 - No help, no way!

Un-noticeably, Mrs. Clara's girls were already in Ty's living room cleaning like the hazmat crew. Uncle David and Andrew had removed the broken windows and measured for the new ones, as well as, Nana's new door. Mrs. Clara swept the shattered glass from the front steps as her girls finished cleaning Ty's suite. Everything was as it had been.

The rest of the family had finished their breakfast and was relaxing in their rooms. Nana was in the kitchen with Judith and Chef, humming and sipping her coffee.

Ty and Steven ate in her kitchen and were relaxing on the sectional. Sissy's healing gift was so good; Ty had no marks, not even a bruise.

Steven had his feet up on the ottoman and Ty was right by his side, dressed in her tie-dyed blue and white halter maxi dress and her Roman white sandals. Just to look at them together they were the dynamic duo.

Steven is all man, but for Ty, he was a gentle, loving, teddy bear and Ty a very feminine but fierce female Warrior. Ty stood five feet seven to Steven six foot five. She was one hundred and fifty pounds built like an African Warrior with long legs, medium breast, a small waist, and medium hips. Her skin was a lovely caramel brown and thick long loose black spiral curls fell to the small of her back. That was the way the Montague women looked and don't forget they all have those piercing gray eyes.

She completed Steven and he balanced her. Steven respected Ty's intelligence, her sensitivity, and her emotional makeup as a woman. She lifted him to be the best head of the household, protector, and provider he could be. They were the best of friends and no one or thing came between them. There was no foolishness, no perverted thoughts, only love and respect as two family members working together for the good of this family and soon their universal family. But now it was time to discuss The Inevitable.

***

"It's time we discuss the plan," Steven said.

"Let's get clear on what we can't do. We can't go to any so-called authorities; they would never listen. They would really think we were a bunch of nuts." Ty explained.

"True that Ty. We can't fight SI's might. We can give people a warning to get out and if they need assistance we can give it." Steven added.

"Uncle David and my father have to build a levy. I know you said a building doesn't make a family, but our family members are buried on this land and we have taken responsibility for all other lives on this property." Ty said.

"I agree and don't you worry. They will build it strong and no harm will come to anyone on this land." He said.

"Steven is that a part of your gift, to know these things?" Ty asked.

"Ty when you get your gift, you will know what I know." He said.

"Why do you keep saying when I get mine?" Ty asked.

"Let it go…and just trust me. Ok! Now back to what we can do." Steven said with closure.

"Do I have a choice?" Ty asked.

Ty was pouting and it didn't go unnoticed by Steven. He scooped her up and hugged her and she gave him a kiss on the cheek.

"You wise old owl! Ok Steven, back to what we can do." Ty said.

"Ty the runway, hangar, and helipad will be first. That should take six weeks. Then the levy another six weeks, that's exactly three months.

When will the plane and chopper be ready?" Steven asked.

"The chopper in one month and the Jet two months," Ty answered.

"Ok, we'll finish the helipad and Captain Devin and Cordell can go take delivery of the Helicopter, then they can get the Jet. We are going to use the chopper, Chef, and the family. I know we have the strength and the stamina to do this." Steven said with confidence.

"We slide in and out," Ty added.

"Yes, that's the way we do business. In and out. We don't do it for the recognition or the glory. Ty they got NO Help. Now we can't stop the storms or the deaths, the crimes, we are not SI. But no fucking way do they get NO help!" Steven said in sheer anger.

"I have Fraternity brothers and you have Sorority sisters. You have friends in the business as well."

"So after we call them and get it cracking, then we have done all we can do and we just have to accept that. But we do not sit on our asses and do nothing." Steven said with conviction.

"Steven calm down. I'm with you." Ty said.

"I'm sorry Ty. Just think I saw it once and it messed me up. I understand why you didn't want to sleep and dream this over and over again," He said.

"I think the sooner we show the family, the sooner we can take care of business. I mean the Montague family and all others involved with the plan. The spouses wouldn't believe it but Nana's children know everything about our gifts and they will get it." Ty said.

"Well, after dinner we'll have a meeting with them and our staff, which includes Chef, Mrs. Clara minus her girls and definitely our pilots. We have work to do!" Steven said.

***

Chapter 20 - Family Business

All the Montagues had made it in. There was Aunt Pam and her husband Bruce aka Daddy Bruce, Aunt Ruthie and her husband John, Uncle David, Uncle DW and his wife Bootsy and Uncle Andrew. All were present and no one was happier than Nana.

Chef had prepared another delicious meal and the family was satisfied. Prior to dinner, Ty had spent some time with her father Andrew and Steven had re-assured him they were a team and they would take care of each other. Andrew felt at ease but soon everyone's mood would quickly change.

They were all at the dinner table when Steven stood up and made the announcement:

"I hate to break up this joyful setting, however, Ty and I need to speak to all Nana's children in the library. This includes Sissy, Kip, Dennis, Chef, Captain Devin, Cordell and Mrs. Clara minus her girls." Steven said as he had omitted Judith and Mrs. Clara's girls on purpose.

They all left the table, excused themselves from their spouses and entered the library as Steven closed the door behind them. Nana's children knew a call to arms when they heard it and this was one of those times.

Steven wasted no time and got right to the point.

"We have a major problem, well actually two! If you all close your eyes I will shoot you a *mental* vision of what it is." He said.

Without a word, everyone closed their eyes and it started like a movie.

Nana's and Dan's story, Ty and Steven on top of the trailer, all of it! One after the other they opened their eyes and gazed at Steven and Ty in a state of disbelief. There were no questions. They knew the when, where and the how. Uncle DW went to the bar and poured himself a drink and Aunt Ruthie told him she needed one too. Uncle David had his hands up on his head, like the thinking man, and Steven walked over and put his hand on his father's shoulder.

"It's my home," Uncle David said with defeat in his voice.

Aunt Pam was at Nana's side, rubbing her back. Ty kneeled down in front of her father and looked at him eye to eye.

"Dad, we need you to build the best damn levee you can to protect Nana's property and every soul that resides on this land, especially you and Uncle David's wives remains," Ty said.

Andrew looked at his daughter with a smile in his eyes, stood up went over to his brother David and pounded his fist.

"We can do that!" they said in unison.

Ty looked at Steven and they smiled.

"Captain Devin and Cordell in six weeks we will have a completed Helipad, Runway, and Hangar. Cordell we"re going to need you to be chopper ready to get us in and out. Can you handle that?" Steven asked.

Smiling with his Uncle Devin by his side, "we got this!" Cordell said.

"That's what I like to hear!" Steven said with a smile.

Steven turned and looked at Chef.

"Chef, you have got to come up with a menu of non-perishables that will hold them for a while and Mrs. Clara you and your girls will help him to pack them when the time is right. You have three months remember that. Aunt Pam and Daddy Bruce, we need Crystal. She's young, strong and we need her help. Kip, Sissy, and Dennis we need you as always." Steven said to all of them.

"I'm down as usual." said Kip.

"Bet!" Dennis added.

"Where you and Ty go...I go!" Sissy said.

Aunt Ruthie just smiled at them. They knew her concern and she knew if she objected, they were grown and made their own decisions. She just prayed for them, loved them, and let them go.

Everyone in the family knew married women would not be asked unless the men couldn't. So Uncle DW's daughters, Carmen, Julie, and Rena, were not asked.

Uncle DW was thankful because he didn't want any strife between him and his wife Bootsy; all five foot two inches of her, with skin the color of sweet brown sugar, long thick black tresses and a smile that was brighter than Ty's eyes. Her eyes would cut deep into uncle DW's soul if he did something she didn't like. But Bootsy had her own blessing, she could sing like an angel. She had one of those voices that could get the attention of God.

All of them loved to hear Bootsy sing and her laugh is a mix of sweetness and devilment. Everything was just right for her personality, and Nana was very pleased when uncle DW brought her home with him for Nana's approval.

Steven had been listening to Uncle DW's thoughts and smiled and shook his head.

"Amazing, you and your wife are still like honeymooners after thirty years," Steven said out loud.

They shook hands and Uncle DW stood up and they did the brother hug.

Aunt Pam knew Crystal was grown, headstrong and the decision was hers and it was going to be yes! However, Pam's other daughters were not asked. Jacqueline was married and the mother of two and even though Aleisha was single, she was hard at work getting her doctorate and Steven decided not to ask her. Ty knew that Aleisha's gift would be as an educator and she agreed with Steven.

All this time, Nana was watching Steven and Ty. She never said a word, she didn't worry. She knew it was horrible as to what was going to happen, but she knew these two had worked together and used their family resources. They had a plan and it was in motion. Nana knew her family would be fine without her. They would carry on, stay close, love and care for each other. That's all she ever wanted!

And now Ty and Steven were thinking and caring for their less fortunate brothers and sisters. Nana couldn't keep the smile off her face.

As the room cleared, everyone knew what they had to do and tomorrow they would be off and running.

Chapter 21 – Family ties – We got work to do

It was early morning and Uncle David and his brother Andrew were surveying the land. Ty's father had his men back-hoeing the helipad as him, David and Daddy Bruce went into town to get extra workers and get windows and a door for the house. They needed extra men to work the fish hatchery, butchers for the livestock and field workers for the gardens.

Uncle DW and Aunt Pam were in the office with Steven and Ty handling the legalities and setting up payroll for the extra workers.

Judith had been helping Mrs. Carla's girls as they were acting squeamish with the chickens. They like to eat them but the process of bringing them to the table was something else. Aunt Bootsy, Ruthie, Nana and Mrs. Clara were also in the barn collecting eggs and getting chickens prepared for freezing.

The Montague's had a designated cellar for freezing meat and vegetable to feed the family. Nana's canning abilities had been passed down to her daughters and soon Ty would learn too. Nana had taught Ty how to make wine and she had ordered wine refrigeration that spread across the left cellar wall. Steven convinced Ty she didn't need more because they were filled to the brim with every type of wine imaginable.

As for Steven, Andrew and David had taught him how to maintenance every operational device on the property. Self-sufficient they are and they would need to be for what was headed their way.

***

Close knit they were. It was just like Nana when her African brothers and sisters lived on this land with her. Bootsy and Ruthie were the best of friends, they even looked like sisters. When DW and John wanted to have a couple's cruise or a get-together, it was always those four and as two couples they are inseparable. Long ago when they lived next door to each other in Ohio, Kip, Sissy, and Dennis spent a lot of time with Bootsy and DW. Especially when John and Ruthie went to Harlem to interview for their teaching positions.

It was a sad day when they left Ohio to live in Harlem. But when Sissy was old enough she returned to Ohio to live. Kip moved to Manhattan, but Dennis stayed in Harlem with his mother and father. Not even distance could separate Bootsy and Ruthie.

Uncle David never wanted to be too far from his mother, ever since his wife passed away. He loves New Orleans, the jazz, blues, the supper clubs, live bands, the people and the food. Uncle David was a New Orleans kind of guy and Steven grew up there and graduated from LSU with honors.

As for Aunt Pam, she married while attending college in Ohio. Shortly after, she moved to Chatta-nooga, where her husband grew up. Her family has been there ever since. Daddy Bruce made good and started his own trucking company.

Uncle Andrew put down roots in Cleveland

and after Ty graduated from Ohio State, she kept it moving. After fifteen years of working in the industry, she decided she wanted her own. She moved to Florida because she needed the sunshine to energize her. But every summer growing up, she spent with her cousins and Nana. Nana was home, ever since her mother passed away, Nana was always home.

***

"I'm headed outside because Dad, Uncle Andrew, and Daddy Bruce just pulled up with five trucks of workers," Steven said.

"That sounds like my husband. If you don't watch him he'll be out there on the grill." Pam laughed.

"What I wouldn't give for his fat burgers."

"Damn Auntie, you married a brother that grill! Ok, you guys got this; I'm going out and do some physical labor." Steven said as he ran out the door.

"I'm with Steven. You two ladies can handle this." Uncle DW said as he left out in a hurry.

Pam and Ty waited till they knew the men were gone before they started their private conversation.

"Ty I want to ask you something," Pam said.

"Sure Auntie," Ty said.

"Out of all my daughters, why Crystal?" Pam asked.

"Don't get me wrong," Ty said with a smile.

"Jacqueline has turned out to be one tough cookie, but she's no Crystal. Aleisha is tough too, but I don't want her to have to make a choice."

"Crystal doesn't need to choose, she just does it. We're going into a closed area with criminals, rapist, thieves and helpless people."

"That's why Crystal. She has a beautiful, compassionate heart but she's a fighter. So if I'm going thru hell, I want Crystal on my side. Just because she's petite and pretty, she's not a pushover. Didn't Aleisha nickname her Scrappy? Well, Scrappy is a Warrior; she's a ride or die chick. If it makes you feel better, Crystal and I will roll into New Orleans together. She'll have my back and I'll have hers." Ty said.

"Now I'm worried about anyone that messes with you and Scrappy!" Pam said as they both let loose of the tension and laughed.

***

For three months the Montague estate was buzzing with people as they finished the work.

Captain Devin and Cordell were very pleased and confident with their flying machines, as Nana called them. Chef was doing Chef and Mrs. Clara and her girls were back to normal. In the evenings, Nana and her children would relax and enjoy themselves as Nana told embarrassing stories about each of them when they were babies. Three months passed by quickly when you're working with a purpose.

***

Chapter 22 – Crystal aka Scrappy

Steven and Ty were going on a flight to Chattanooga Tennessee to pick up Crystal, aka Scrappy. Kip, Dennis, and Sissy were coming along for the first flight of the new MTQ1. Chef had stocked the galley with beverages and his surprise lunch.

Cordell was more excited than Captain Devin

about the flight. Captain Devin loved to fly and this was the first time he was able to pick what he wanted; a Jet specifically made for him. Proud yes, this was his Jet and he knew it.

Captain Devin just loved the new MTQ1, and Cordell just sat at her console and shook his head. Never, ever in his wildest dreams would he have a Jet like this to co-pilot and his own helicopter with all his specifications. As far as Cordell and Captain Devin were concerned, yes they were proud, thankful and they were never leaving. This was their new home, this was their purpose.

***

Nana and her children were on the front porch watching as they saw the Jet lift off; rise up to the heavens and then it was gone. "Ooh child, that's some kind of flying machine. Those babies are full of won-der and surprise." Nana stated.

"You think we'll get to fly with them in that machine?" Judith asked.

"Ooh, most definitely child, sooner than you think. That's something else to be up in the heavens with Si." Nana said with a smile.

***

"Good morning this is your Captain speaking. Feel free to move about the cabin and please take a look out your window. It's a beautiful day that God has made. Thank you, Jesus! We will reach our desti-nation in two hours; enjoy your flight aboard the new MTQ1." Captain Devin announced with pride.

The Montague family clapped and cheered as Captain Devin and Cordell smiled at each other and gave the brother pound.

They released their seatbelts and looked out the windows. It really was a beautiful day SI had made, Thank you, God Almighty.

**

Sissy and Ty headed straight to the gallery.

"Ty, would you look at this! Chef stocked the bar, made us gumbo and crab meat po'boys. Girl, we have a homemade German chocolate cake." Sissy squealed.

"Sis, if he doesn't stop, my ass is going to be as big as the tail end of this Jet," Ty said as they both cackled with laughter.

Sissy and Ty poured themselves a glass of Nana's red grape wine and started playing stewardess for everyone on board, including Captain Devin and Cordell. They were fifteen minutes away from the airport and Captain Devin made his announcement for landing. The MTQ1 landed on a dime, without a hitch!

They taxied down the runway and Crystal saw the Jet from the glass hallway.

"My family, just look at us, MTQ1," she said with her sweet, but bad ass little voice.

When the Jet parked and the pilots opened the door, the automatic stairs lowered and the two regal pilots exited first. Dennis and Kip were next. Sissy, Ty, and Steven were last.

As the Montagues entered the airport, Crystal ran and jumped into Kip's arms. She was a little something but she thought she was much bigger. Crystal stood four foot five, one hundred and five pounds. Her hair was cut in a sleek bob and like all of them; she had those Montague gray eyes.

Kip passed her to Dennis who passed her to

Steven, as she squealed and, laughed and gave them hugs and kisses.

"Put her down Steven. I'm not about to pick her up and have my ovaries fall out and roll across the floor," Sissy said.

Sissy and Ty fell out laughing!

"Some of the shit Sissy says is just too funny," Ty said.

"Now ain't your cousins fine, child?" Sissy asked Crystal.

"As all hell! And the Jet..." Crystal said laughing out loud.

"Crystal you know that's Ty's ass. Ooh Tybama of the United Black States of America," Sissy said laughing.

Ty was standing there with a smile/smirk on her face.

"Get your little self over here and give me some love. Don't let Sissy get you beat down. She's in heat and needs a man." Ty fired back.

Ty and Crystal embrace and laughed.

"Oh, she needs some Vitamin D." Crystal laughed.

Ty was laughing so hard she could barely speak.

"Four times a day for life." said Ty.

Sissy was speechless and that was a first.

"Let's head to the bar, get something to drink and we can talk," Ty said.

As the Montagues headed off; Devin and Cordell were standing so tall and looking so good in their spotless pilot suits. They notice the ladies were smiling at them as they smiled back and strutted to the pilot's lounge.

They would have to wait till the necessary maintenance checks were done before they were clear for takeoff.

***

As they finished their family conversation, they heard the overhead announcement: "The MTQ1 was ready for boarding."

They walked up to the Jet to board, and Captain Devin and Cordell were on the left and right of the stairs.

"I just love a man in uniform," Sissy said.

"It makes me proud to see two beautiful African American pilots fly this beautiful Jet. I'm proud as hell!" Ty said.

"Me too Ty and so are they. Just look at them. It's truly a sight to see." Sissy added.

As the last Montague entered the Jet their

pilots entered and Cordell operated the mechanical stair lift until the door sealed itself into place. He joined Captain Devin in the cockpit and they ran their system checks, taxied to the runway and smoothly lifted off up to the heavens, headed home to Nana's.

***

As they landed on their new custom runway, Steven and Ty looked at each other and thanked SI for all the wonderful people he had given them. Nana and the family were waiting for them as the Jet taxied to a stop. Crystal was greeted by her mother and father as she reassured them she would be alright in New Orleans with Ty. Everyone loaded into the white golf carts and headed towards the mansion. As soon as they hit the door, they could smell and see that Chef had laid out dinner. He made the announcement and they all piled into their seats and dined sufficiently.

After dinner, Steven announced to the family it was time to go over the plans. They needed to talk it out one last time before heading out tomorrow. Everyone met on the porch outside.

There were no questions and everyone understood what they had to do. It was a get in and get out mission. Simple! But there were always variables to the best-laid plans and the Montagues knew that better than anyone.

***

Chapter 23- New Orleans, day one (Sunday)

T he mayor was considering announcing a man-datory evacuation to the Superdome and the Montagues were loading every eighteen wheeler Daddy Bruce owned, and he owned many. Nana said the family is your greatest resource and Steven had a plan.

They had modified the engines intakes to a

pipe that ran to the top of the rigs. So the rigs would have to be completely submerged to stall out.

They modified the front grills with padded bumpers to move anything aside as they blazed a trail. They had welded metal undercarriages to stop anything from going up under them and hindering motion.

Chef had made non-perishable foods: smoked meats, fresh fruits, and nuts, homemade peanut butter, crackers and yeast bread.

They had cases of bottled water, sanitary products, disposable toothbrushes, aspirins, bandages, diapers for infants and the elderly, feminine products, infant formula, juices and plastic baby bottles, plastic fork, spoons, knives, easy open can goods, napkins and toilet paper, clean white t-shirt, socks, lotions, deodorants, wipes, hand sanitizers, self-inflatable beds, any and everything they could think of was in those trailers and on them!

Steven insisted everyone wore dark military fatigues made out of water resistant material, inflatable vest, hats, boots and dark aviator glasses. They were packed up and ready to pull out when the mayor called for evacuation.

Even though the winds were howling and the rain was strong and swinging debris around, their modified rigs were hauling ass straight to the Superdome.

They went down the congested highway pushing abandon cars and trucks out the way. They pushed trees and down lights out of the way. No one questioned them when the rigs pulled in, after all, they looked like the military and they had supplies!

Before they could exit the trucks, the people

were on them. They were smiling and thanking God that someone came to help! As Crystal and Ty exited her father's truck they could see the multitude of people stranded there.

They were poor, white and African American. It made no difference; they were just people and all the Montagues cared. They gave a damn and would do what they could to help. Like Sissy said, "If we treat others like we were treated, we would be no better than them." So they helped everyone!

And like them, there would be many others to do the same; from the common man to the celebrities. Many people cared and would help as they could.

The government couldn't get their shit together, couldn't agree, didn't have a clue and no Brownie your ass did not do a good job, Mr. Fema man!

The governor had her head in the clouds; turning down help. Well, after all, it wasn't her and her family suffering out there!

***

Steven was just about to call it a wrap when an elderly man approached him about his sister being sent to another makeshift shelter. He knew they needed supplies and since he wanted to be with her, he would show them the way.

"Ok everyone, we've done all we can here but there's one more stop we didn't know about. So everyone follow us," Steven said.

The team acknowledged him and began to follow. They went several miles out the way to find the makeshift shelter. When they got there they found the same despair. Children, infants and the elderly, more overcrowding and no one had brought them a thing.

These sweet people were so grateful; they hugged everyone and thanked them all, except Crystal.

"Where the hell are you Crystal?" Ty said *mentally* and Steven heard Ty.

"Ty, hurry I'm down this way," Crystal replied.

Without a thought, Ty did a full out run in Crystal's direction.

"Ty stop, I'll go get her," Steven said.

"I promised her mother I would take care of her, besides, I'm almost there. Steven the wind and the rain, it's getting worse." Ty said.

"I know, but I'm not leaving without you," Steven said.

Ty had reached Crystal. She was in an old two story house trying to free an elderly woman from the falling beams that pinned her against the wall. And even worse, the woman was trying to keep her two grandsons above the rising water. They were two little, beautiful baby boys, maybe three months old, twins!

They couldn't swim and couldn't help their grandmother. Thank SI, Crystal had heard the woman cry out to God almighty for help, and he sent it.

"Get the babies, C!" Ty screamed.

As Crystal got the two babies, Ty had just enough time to throw herself on top of the woman when the ceiling gave way. The water had risen quickly with the roof caving down to the first-floor level. It quickly got to four feet high inside the house and all the while, Steven had been calling Ty, but she never answered.

***

Against his will and Uncle Andrew and Daddy Bruce, it was time to make the call. They had to leave them! The wind and rain were increasing, and Steven had to do the unthinkable!

"I can't reach Ty, we don't know where they are and we have to go back. The hurricane is coming and there's a 6:00 pm curfew. I don't want to see this end this way, but we have got to go. I trust Ty and I know they will make it." Steven said.

There was not one single word said between them as they headed away from downtown, without Crystal and Ty.

Steven knew the male DNA was strong and he and Sissy had received their gifts, but not Ty. Out of all of them, she was the weakest link. It was her nightmare not his. Was this her fate? As strong as Steven was, he had never had to make a decision like this. But Nana knew all about tragedies and facing the fact that some things were just inevitable.

Nana had heard every word and she knew it was time for the family to pray.

***

"I need for everyone to link as I pray to SI," Nana said.

"Dear Heavenly Father, we come to you to ask you for strength to deal with the inevitable. Please help those in need. Open hearts SI, and round up your people to help our earthly brothers and sisters. Fill us with hope and courage to persevere through these times and if it's your will, please bring our loved ones back home safely. Thank you SI, Amen." Nana concluded *mentally* and everyone said:

Amen!

Prepare yourself!

As sure as there is life, there is

death.

The Inevitable!

The second book of The Learning.

Be sure to check in at www.TheLearningNovels.com.

I'll share insight and preview "The Inevitable."

Meet me at the "Author's Corner" and share your thoughts on "Let's Talk."

Be seeing you soon, Ty